9/1/21

Please return/renew this item by the
last date shown to avoid a charge.
Books may also be renewed by phone
and Internet. May not be renewed if
required by another reader.

www.libraries.barnet.gov.uk

LONDON BOROUGH

THE INVISIBLE LAND

The Invisible Land

Hubert Mingarelli

Translated from the French
by Sam Taylor

GRANTA

Granta Publications, 12 Addison Avenue, London W11 4QR

First published in Great Britain by Granta Books, 2020

First published in French as *La Terre Invisible*
by Libella, Paris, 2019

This book is supported by the Institut français
(Royaume-Uni) as part of the Burgess programme.

A CIP catalogue record is available from the British Library

2   4   6   8   9   7   5   3   1

ISBN 978 1 78378 602 2
eISBN 978 1 78378 604 6

www.granta.com

Typeset in Bembo by Patty Rennie

Printed and bound by CPI Group (UK) Ltd,
Croydon, CR0 4YY

THE INVISIBLE LAND

Germany, July 1945

FOR NEARLY TWO weeks of that hot July I waited in Dinslaken, on the banks of the Rhine. I couldn't make up my mind to leave, even though I'd photographed everything there was to photograph. Each day the sun was white and the night brought no relief from the heat. It was suffocating, day and night. I didn't know why I stayed on. I spent most of my time in the hotel since I had hardly any money left. In the morning I went down to see the river and in the evening I sat on the bench in Dürenstrasse. I closed my eyes and waited for the heat to abate a little before I went back to the hotel.

I heard footsteps, and he appeared from behind the bench like a ghost, carrying a cardboard box full of beer bottles. He sat next to me for a while, then we drank and we talked and he got up. He stood with his legs astride and his mouth wide open as if he were eating the air. He wrote for a Dutch newspaper. Behind him, the sun set over a mountain of red bricks. The rubble was being sorted through and piled up in various places. 'And you?' he asked. I took my camera from my pocket and he said: 'Ah, right.' The sun dazzled me and now it was dancing on his legs. I didn't know where he'd found all those beers. 'I don't have anything else to say,' he told me. 'I've already seen it all. My head's full of it. I'm leaving tomorrow.' He sat back down next to me. He smelled of sweat and beer. One hour before, he'd been a stranger. We watched the sun sink towards the river, invisible from here, and when it had disappeared the sky grew dark. We could hear noises but we didn't know where they were coming from. In the distance, an engine that wouldn't start. I closed my eyes for a moment and, when I opened them again, he wasn't there. A woman in soldier's boots walked past, pushing a handcart with nothing on it. Her dress was an immaculate white. The wheel creaked. A star lit up the sky. In the distance the engine finally started. Two beers and everything was mysterious.

THE WOMAN IN soldier's boots was at the end of the street, sitting on the handcart in the darkness. She was talking to herself and she didn't see me go past. As I walked through the dark streets I thought about her and, at one point, the beer still working its magic, I wanted to go back and photograph what she was saying. Then in the distance I saw the hotel windows, still lit up, and the Union Jack flapping from a first-floor window like a sheet hung out to dry. The sentry leaning against the entrance nodded at me. When I said 'Goodnight', he shook his head, as if at a joke. I went upstairs and, inside my room, knocked on the wall to let Colonel Collins know that I was back. I lay down on the bed. I didn't have to wait long. He came in, braces dangling over his hips. He was sweating profusely and in the darkness he looked intimidating. In daylight, though, he had a gentle face, and he looked thoughtfully at things and at men. While he waited to go home to Wales, he was in the charge of the town here. He and his men had set up their office in the local gymnasium, the only large building still standing. I had followed him and his engineer regiment from the French border to Bavaria, and since we'd been in Dinslaken he had come to my room almost every night. He was an amateur photographer. We talked about photography and sometimes about the bridges that he built before the war. He took a chair, sat down, and placed a bowl of cherries on the bed. 'Everything here comes through me,' he said, 'even cherries.' We started eating them. He had never seen my photographs, but he knew the newspapers I worked for. I had never seen his photographs either. He stood up and went to the window to throw away his cherry stones. Then he remained there, facing the night.

I told him about the woman with the handcart. I said that I'd wanted to photograph what she was saying, but I didn't mention the two beers I'd drunk. He turned around, reached a hand towards me and, with the black sky behind him, tried to tell me something. But he couldn't, so he leaned out of the window and talked to the sentry: 'How's it going down there? Where are you from, lad?' I couldn't hear the sentry's answer. The colonel looked at his watch and said: 'One more hour to go. Hang in there!' Then he added a phrase that all his men had heard him say at least once and which they probably thought was a joke: 'Love God, my boy – the

6

time will pass more quickly.' He sat back down again and ate some more cherries. This time he threw the stones out of the window from where he was sitting. 'They all ask me for something,' he said. 'But I make them understand that there's a time to keep their mouths shut. If they start crying to soften me up, I'm afraid I'll lose my temper.' He missed the window, stood up, found the stone, threw it outside and remained standing there looking out at the night. A plane flew past. 'Today,' he said, 'they came to ask me for shoes. I said: "You think I've opened a shop?" I started laughing and I told them to go away. They started to leave. Then I said: "No, hang on, I remember where there are some, but take a van." I showed them on the map where they could find huge piles of shoes.' At that moment, the plane disappeared. Collins stood in front of the window for a long time without moving, then smiled with false cheer. He sat down and started eating cherries again, throwing the stones into the night, pretending to enjoy himself, thinking that this might hide from me the seething hate that he felt towards the Germans. The hate he bore them was greater than the hate his men felt because they had been able to release it a little by killing large numbers of them, even after they surrendered. And I had photographed large numbers of them too, in whatever grotesque or human positions death had surprised them.

We didn't talk about photography that night, but about the men who were going home. We mentioned their names, remembered their faces, and we shared the same vaguely sad smile when we thought about McFee, the colonel's driver. Then he went away, leaving me the last few cherries, and for a long time I heard him pacing his room, from one wall to the other, utterly alone.

I COULDN'T SLEEP either. I listened to the changing of the guard outside the door, the sentries talking in low voices, and when I got up and went to the window, they waved up at me. I waved back and looked out at the river, so dark from here that it seemed to float between earth and sky, the way I had once seen the blue expanse of a lake float. We had been driving at a crawl for hours that day, the convoy stretched out behind and ahead of us, and suddenly McFee, the driver, started hitting the steering wheel, honking his horn at the truck in front as if it might change anything. Collins, sitting next to him, said gently: 'What's the matter, lad? You in a rush?'

McFee shook his head. 'Sorry, Colonel. Just a habit.'

I was sitting behind Collins and we watched as we slowly approached a lake of the most intense blue. On its bank two Germans lay side by side on their backs, their uniform jackets half hiked up, exposing their bellies, and behind them the calm and intensely blue lake seemed to belong to neither sky nor earth. Collins and McFee paid no attention to the two Germans. In the truck ahead of us the men were playing cards on a petrol can, and after driving alongside the lake we crossed a bridge over the Weser and entered an endless plain. Daylight faded and we heard the rumble of the war in the distance, and the horizon lit up with orange waves as if it were morning.

That evening, sitting under the eaves of a house, I listened to the murmur of the camp we had set up and the truck engines idling to give us electricity. I saw Collins' men coming and going and I heard someone quietly speaking German from a dark window. I saw white sheets fall across windows. Crossing the road, a little girl walked towards me, carefully carrying a helmet as if it were a pan full of boiling water. She sat next to me, and inside the helmet there was a mouse on a bed of straw. I signalled the girl to put down the helmet. I placed a new roll of film in my camera and bent over to take a few photographs. For a long time after, I kept thinking about MacGraw, who developed my photographs for the newspaper, discovering the mouse in the helmet on the same roll of film as the pictures I would take the next day, at almost the same hour.

We set off again at dawn. It was a fine spring day and, until evening, we didn't see any German soldiers, just lots of civilians by the roadside, and as we were driving slowly along McFee raised his hand from the steering wheel and waved to them ceremoniously like George VI and sometimes one of them would solemnly wave back and McFee would burst out laughing and Collins would say nothing, only shake his head, and we kept on like that until evening without hearing a single gunshot, hardly even slowed down by the cars that the trucks ahead of us pushed into the ditches.

I was sitting beside Collins when we entered the camp. Seeing me hesitate, seeing me stop using my camera, he gave me a questioning look while his men advanced between the grey corpses and sometimes crossed themselves and looked at one another and tried to catch Collins' eye without thinking to wrap a scarf around their faces to block out the stench but crouching silently in front of the grey, naked bodies of the dying and they remained there crouching motionless in the evening light and their lips didn't move either and they kept trying to look at Collins, their colonel, but he couldn't think of anything to say to them because he couldn't think of anything at all and suddenly someone sent a flare up above the camp and it fell back to earth lighting up the dead and the living in the same red glow and at that moment nobody thought that the man who'd fired the flare had lost his mind but that he'd sent it up deliberately like a red howl aimed at the sky or a prayer and when it died out it left behind an even deeper silence.

Collins ordered the trucks into the camp and their headlights cast gigantic shadows and the petrol fumes made us cough but at least they protected us from the stench. A grey haze floated above the ground all night and in the morning the wind blew it away. The dead had been covered with tarpaulins. The dying had been carried into the huts and we had covered them with our blankets. Those who could walk stayed outside in groups alongside the huts and they looked up at the still-pale sky as if they could read something in it and they drank from our flasks and slowly ate the bread, the meat, the biscuits from the combat ration packs and the sun rose and we heard wild yells followed by a long burst of gunfire and we saw a sergeant coming towards us shoving a distraught guard ahead of him. 'There were three of them, Colonel.' The sergeant pointed to a wooden cabin near the entrance: two bodies lay across the doorway. 'They were over there. I missed this one. What should I do with him?' He shoved him with the butt of his gun. 'Eh, what should I do? We could always hang him, Colonel. I'll do it – I don't mind.' The survivor groaned. The terror on his face made him look forty. He was sobbing and he rubbed his head with his hand. Blood was trickling down his neck.

Collins was sitting on a bench, leaning against a hut, dark rings around his eyes, and he took his revolver from its holster and pointed it at the sky, just above the prisoner's head. The barrel shook. The sergeant stepped to the side to avoid the trajectory and suddenly Collins put the revolver on the bench, stood up and punched the prisoner in the face then held him in his arms and hit him again and hugged him again and he looked as if he were whispering into the man's ear and, like all the men there at that moment, I thought that he had well and truly lost it. A Russian plane flew over us, waving its wings in greeting. They took the survivor with them. A few days later Collins confided in me in a fit of despair, the only time I ever saw him like that: 'We were all tired, we couldn't see straight any more, and I scared myself.' He broke off and the despair grew bigger. I looked away, and in a whisper he said: 'I have a son and my God I swear . . . I swear that man had his eyes.'

I WAS STILL in front of the window and the sentry who'd been relieved was disappearing into the night. The one who'd stayed behind started to whistle. I leaned down to see him. He was standing motionless in the doorway. I'd heard that tune before.

We were driving towards Dinslaken, where Collins' regiment had been posted. A summer rain was falling, the sun shining through it, and it washed the road and the tarps of the trucks, and soothed me too. McFee was driving, whistling softly. Beside him, Collins watched the fields. I was sitting in the back seat. The war had been over for a month. The roads were clear. Beehives stood in the middle of flowering meadows. Perhaps because of the soothing rain, a flood of images came to me as if in a dream. Suddenly I leaned towards Collins and said, half-asleep and without really thinking: 'Collins, what did we see back there?'

Collins didn't move and he didn't say a word, as if he hadn't heard or was thinking, and after a while McFee

14

turned quickly towards him and his lips moved and I saw a vein throbbing at his temple and there was another long silence filled only by the rain and then suddenly: 'You want my opinion, Colonel?'

'Go ahead.'

'What we saw, I think that . . .'

He said nothing more. He started driving more carefully, looking right and left, and Collins and I waited.

'In fact . . . I don't know, Colonel.' He shook his head and repeated: 'No, I don't know.'

Collins said: 'Nor do any of us, lad. Don't worry about it.'

McFee looked right and left again, for longer this time, and in a voice that he tried to control, said: 'I'm half-Jewish on my mother's side, Colonel.'

Collins turned to him and suddenly the rain stopped. Steam rose from the fields. Two horses looked up at us. In the truck ahead of us, the men lifted the tarp and looked up at the sky. McFee shrugged and he too glanced up at the sky. 'I didn't mind driving in the rain. Where I live, it's like that almost every day. It's like the sea. I'm not making this up, Colonel, I swear. When it rains, it's like the sea.'

Collins murmured: 'We believe you, McFee, we believe you.'

McFee opened his mouth to say something in reply, but in the end he just smiled and went back to driving more casually. Sunlight poured into the car. It dazzled us. In the tall grass of the fields, the beehives looked like towns.

One hour later – an hour in which he had shown no emotion, even whistling at times – McFee slowed to a stop and put on the handbrake. After whispering a few words to Collins, he left the car and, turning away from us, crossed his hands behind the back of his neck and his shoulders shook like two frightened animals. As Collins' car was always in the middle of the convoy when his regiment was on the move, half of the trucks and light armoured vehicles pulled away from us while the other half stopped and waited behind us. A thousand men moving away under the sun after the rain and a thousand waiting for McFee to calm down.

McFee was back home now, with the first demobilised troops, and I wondered if he was sleeping at that moment or if he could hear the rain falling like the sea. I wondered if he'd told his father the same things he'd told his mother and I remembered taking a photograph of him in front of the car a few days before he left, and I wondered if anyone apart from me, looking at that photograph, would be able to read in his eyes what he had seen. At the moment I took it, he looked happy: he was going home.

The sentry stopped whistling. He walked along the street, tossed his cigarette and came back towards the door. A small yellow flame rose from a building with no front wall. Shadows moved around it and while I tried to make them out amid the darkness of the night, an idea that I'd had in Bavaria, then abandoned, came back to me. I thought about it, for something to do. I weighed up the pros and cons. I was about to abandon it again, putting it down to insomnia this time, when I heard Collins get up and start pacing his room. I hesitated, then approached the wall. 'Can I come in, Collins?'

'Come!' he said.

I put on my shoes and went into the corridor. He opened the door. His window overlooked the courtyard: it was darker than mine. A bedside lamp shone on the floor. He sat on his bed and I took a chair. He wiped his neck with a towel.

'I need you, Collins. I need a car.'

'You're going home?'

He looked at me, stunned.

'No, I want to photograph them. If you can't swing it,

17

that's fine. I'll leave tomorrow. I'll send you my photos. We'll write to each other. You can tell me what you think of them. You can send me yours.'

Collins shook his head. He was almost laughing. 'I don't understand. Who are you talking about?'

'The people of this damned country, Collins. I want to photograph them in front of their homes.'

'Why?'

'I don't know yet.'

This time he did laugh. 'I'm the same as you. I talk rubbish when I can't sleep.'

He pointed towards the window.

'Why not the people here? There are plenty of them in the streets. Come to the gymnasium, you'll see some strange ones. Why go so far in a car?'

He was breathing heavily.

'I don't know yet, Collins.'

In a kind voice, he said: 'Then go home.' He stared at me. He blinked and said very slowly: 'We should all go home.'

The lamp on the floor dimmed for a few moments and then lit us brightly from below again. Collins began to move his head back and forth, looking increasingly anxious. I wanted to leave. There was a glimmer of pain in his eyes.

'But we haven't seen everything yet. We're starting to hear

about it. Thousands of them, in ditches, machine-gunned. Ukraine is a graveyard. And who dug the ditches?'

He fell silent, and then whispered: 'How fast did their hearts beat while they were digging?'

I could see his chest swell. His gaze passed over me, then gathering a little strength he said, as if to himself: 'You want to photograph them and you don't know why.'

He smiled vaguely. I said nothing. He picked up the towel again and wiped the sweat from his forehead.

'You won't see anything, you know. I'm sure of it. They are what they are and I want to forget them.'

I waited a moment and then stood up.

'Let's try to get some sleep.'

Back in my room, I went to the window. In the collapsed building, the small flame was still shining, but no shadows moved around it now. Below, the sentry had rested his head against the frame of the door and looked like he was sleeping. Above the river, I recognised a few stars.

I GOT UP late. Not a sound. Collins and his officers had long ago left for the gymnasium. In the corridor, two women were folding a sheet. I went down to the kitchens and asked for some coffee.

On the other side of the table, the fat man who'd served me continued peeling potatoes. He was a sort of odd-job man. We had never exchanged a single word. Occasionally he would glance at me, his face unreadable as if he were checking the time on a clock. I never saw any expression on his face, not this morning nor on any of the other days. There was something repulsive in his empty eyes. I had never heard him speak.

Outside the hotel, the sentry was looking for some shade. I walked down the street to the square where the theatre used to be. There were some huts made from wood and cor-rugated iron there now, and I turned onto the avenue that led to the Rhine. Bricks were piled up everywhere. Clouds of white dust floated from one pavement to the other, mingling with smoke from fires where people cooked food. On the ground, sheets were covered with objects saved from the flames, laid out for sale. Women lined up with buckets in front of a water pipe. Old men dozed in wicker chairs. The river appeared, dark blue, as wide as an estuary.

On the bank where I usually went, a horse was being butchered. I wandered off and sat on a large stone. The river moved past with many things floating in it, all tangled together. I took out my camera, looked through the view-finder at these strange rafts, and – since I'd decided to leave – took a picture to remind me of this final day.

Going back up the avenue under the noon sun, my deci-sion made, I felt lightened. Outside the gymnasium, two sentries were listening uncomprehendingly to a woman dressed in her Sunday best. As I walked past, she grabbed my arm and spoke to me. I shook my head, freed myself from her grip and went inside. German secretaries sat behind typewriters on restaurant tables. French and British officers smoked, bent over a map. At the back, under the largest window, Collins sat at his desk, hands behind his neck, talking to a sergeant, and when the sergeant moved away I went over to tell him that I was leaving and to ask whether I could get a seat on a cargo plane. Collins smiled and shook his head.

'They want me to hang the prosecutor and I suppose he deserves it, but I'm not going to do that. I don't care if it's in the rules or not. They can hang him somewhere else.' Laughing, he added: 'I told them I didn't have any carpenters in my regiment. They won't believe it, but who cares?'

He unlocked his hands and rubbed his cheeks.

'My God, I didn't sleep long. I didn't have time to shave this morning either, but I found your car. Shame McFee already left. Come on!'

I followed him towards three orderlies leaning against a wall, dressed in new uniforms with second-class stripes. Seeing Collins, they stood to attention. Collins said to the first one: 'What's your name, lad?'

'O'Leary, Colonel.'

'How long have you been here?'

'Two weeks, Colonel.'

'Can you drive?'

'Yes.'

'There's a car behind the gymnasium. Get it running and find a flag to hang on it.'

'Which flag, Colonel?'

'Montenegro, lad. Why not?'

The two other orderlies burst out laughing. O'Leary grimaced and rolled his eyes. Collins smiled good-heartedly.

'We'll get you a road map. You're going on detachment for a few days. Take your weapon and pack a bag, lad, and tell your company commander to come and see me.'

O'Leary started to blush and Collins was about to say something else when we heard someone yelling. It was the woman in the elegant dress. She'd managed to get inside and she was begging the two sentries, who were pushing her towards the door. Collins turned in their direction and when her yelling died down he headed for his desk, leaving me with O'Leary, who stared at me, trying to work out who I was and what on earth all that nonsense with the flag was about.

I LEFT THE gymnasium with O'Leary and went to see the car. We walked around it. He didn't know how to address me and seemed terrified by this large, shiny, pale green car. He opened the door, sat behind the wheel, and for a moment he sat there without moving. Then he looked up at me, bewildered. 'Are we going?'

'Yes.'

He put the car in neutral, lifted the handbrake and started the engine. He stared at me again. His hair was cut so short that I could see his scalp.

'And where are we going?'

I said as if to myself: 'I don't know yet.'

He turned off the engine and while we walked back to the gymnasium I explained to him that I wasn't an officer but a photographer. He still didn't understand what was happening, but he seemed to relax a little. I left him at the entrance. As I walked away, I heard him running up behind me.

'Which flag, sir?'

'The Union Jack.'

He walked back to the gymnasium, shoulders slightly stooped. In the hotel, I saw the fat odd-job man in the corridor and told him I was leaving for several days. His unfathomable gaze passed over me. I didn't care whether he'd understood or not.

In the room I packed my bag and lay on my bed, covered in sweat, until a low-flying plane made me vaguely sad, and while the roar of its engines faded I closed my eyes and decided to wait at least an hour, enough time for O'Leary to find a flag. I fell asleep and dreamed about the tarpaulins that we'd spread over the dead that night, and in my dream they lifted up and we thought it was the wind and even though we hammered stakes into the ground to hold them down they still kept lifting up. We held them down with our hands, using all our strength, but a greater force continued to lift them up and each of us knew deep down that it was the dead, pushing at the tarpaulins with their grey legs.

I started awake, picked up my bag and walked back to the gymnasium, thinking about this dream, which never really changed. There was always the problem of the tarpaulin that wouldn't properly cover the dead, and the way we kept inventing excuses for that failure. There was the wind, the stakes that broke, there was always something, because nobody dared admit that it was the dead pushing at the tarp with their legs.

I wanted to see Collins before I left, but he wasn't there. O'Leary was waiting for me by the car, rifle at his shoulder. He'd stuck the flag into one of the back windows. He opened the boot for me. I put my bag in with his, between a crate full of ration packs, three jerry cans and two regulation blankets.

'What should I do with the rifle? Boot or back seat?'

'Whatever you want.'

He put it on the back seat and looked around. Once we were inside the car, he turned to me. A vein was pulsing at his temple.

'Tell me where I should go.'

'Let's try to get out of here first.'

He started the car and, while he was manoeuvring it, I asked where he was from.

'My mother lives near Lowestoft.'

We left the gymnasium behind us and he turned onto a street that looked open all the way. We drove between piles of bricks. 'Lowestoft? That's near the sea, isn't it?'

'Yes, sir. It's at the seaside.'

We lowered the windows. The hot air blew in, and a smell of burning. We moved away from the town centre and now there were a few almost undamaged houses between the piles of stones and concrete beams, then there were warehouses, a water mill, wooden huts, and suddenly nothing. We were driving between fields and orchards. At the top of a hill, we caught one last glimpse of the Rhine. In the distance ahead there was a flash of heat lightning.

O'LEARY DROVE CAREFULLY in the middle of the road, slowing down whenever a pothole appeared and avoiding almost all of them. The flag, precariously trapped between the windowpane and the frame, flapped against the glass. We moved between empty fields and the horizon clouded over.

'If you're not an officer, I can ask you questions.'

'You can, yes.'

'So you don't know where we're going, okay, but if we're going anyway, there must be a reason, right?'

There was no irony in his voice, only curiosity and a glimmer of anxiety. At that moment the flag stopped flapping. I turned around: it had vanished. 'Stop!'

I found it in a bush, folded it up and put it on the back seat. We set off again. Soon after that, O'Leary spoke again. 'So . . . the reason?'

I hesitated, and said: 'My work, O'Leary. I'm going to take photographs.'

He nodded vaguely, then looked out at the road and the

sky where large clouds were rolling towards us, illuminated by the lightning. O'Leary started slowing down and said dreamily: 'That's no ordinary storm. I think we should stop.'

We saw rooftops, quite far ahead. The storm broke as we were approaching them and O'Leary parked the car under the eaves of a hay barn. We stayed in our seats listening to the rain and when the storm passed by we kept waiting. Then the sun reappeared behind a cloud of mist.

A woman came out of the house opposite the barn and, when she saw us, went back inside. Soon after, a middle-aged man appeared. I got out of the car. He approached through the mist and spoke in a booming, surprised voice. But I interrupted him, and he must have realised I was speaking a foreign language because he stared at me in mute astonishment and crossed his arms. I hadn't planned to do it here, but I took the camera from my pocket and using sign language I explained my intention to photograph him and his family. He shrugged and walked back slowly towards the house. For an instant I wondered what to do, then I leaned down to the car.

'Come on, O'Leary. And give me your road map.'

He got out of the car and handed me a brown envelope. I joined the man outside his front door, opened the envelope and showed him the sheet of paper with the military letterhead. He bent over it, looked up, saw O'Leary and blushed a little. Again using sign language, I explained what I wanted to do. He glanced at the sky, turned around and called out in his deep voice. The woman came out and he whispered a few words to her. She was much younger than him. I took a few steps back, signalled them to turn towards me, and just as I was about to take the picture a little girl in an embroidered dress appeared at the door. The man spoke gently to her and the girl started to move away. I made him understand that she should stand between them. The man held out his hand, and when she was in place I pressed the button. The woman and the girl immediately went back inside. The man didn't move. As I walked to the car, I noticed that I was trembling slightly and it wasn't as hot.

We started driving between empty fields again and soon there wasn't a trace of water on the road. O'Leary let his hand sail in the wind outside. We began to make out the bluish line of a forest.

'I'm in the Signals, but I like driving too.'

DAYLIGHT WAS FADING as we entered the forest. Large ferns grew on either side of the road and the trees were so tall that it felt like we were driving through the night. We passed a truck loaded with wood. O'Leary stopped the car while he worked out how to turn on the headlights. The truck brushed past us with a blast of air. We set off again and it was strange, that straight line between the trees: the headlights seemed to illuminate it all the way to the end, but we never got there.

The road divided into several narrower roads. We took the middle one, but fairly soon it became a forest path. We turned back, and at the crossroads O'Leary asked: 'What should I do? Which way now?'

I got out of the car. I could hear hundreds of frogs in the deep night. I bent down to O'Leary. 'May as well stay here.' I pointed to a clearing among the trees. He manoeuvred the car into the ferns and turned off the headlights. I was still on the road. I thought about the little girl and her embroidered dress. O'Leary came towards me, rifle at his shoulder.

'Are you afraid someone will steal it?'

'No, I'm not afraid. It's regulations.'

We went back to the car. Sitting on the edge of the boot, we opened our ration packs. O'Leary looked pensive as he ate, glancing up at the sky, which was only just visible between the treetops. He drank from his flask and passed it to me. The water was lukewarm. The singing of the frogs went on and on.

'This morning we were talking in the gymnasium about how bored we all were and what we'd be doing tomorrow, and now I'm eating here and it's less hot. I'm going to sleep outside, next to the car. I'll make a mattress from the ferns. That doesn't bother me. In Lowestoft, where I lived, I used to go and sleep on the dunes.'

He was staring at his shoes and talking for the sake of talking, I could tell.

'Were you called up or did you volunteer?'

'Volunteered, but I wanted to ask you. That photo you took earlier, what was it for?'

'Nothing in particular. I just felt like it.'

'In Lowestoft, when I used to sleep on the dunes, I'd look at the sea because I just felt like it.'

We drank a can of grape juice. The night full of songs consoled me. We got ready to go to sleep. O'Leary cut a load of ferns with his knife and spread his blanket over them. I lay on the back seat, the bag under my head, my legs folded, and through the open window I asked: 'How's your bed of ferns?'

'Pretty comfortable. Goodnight, sir.'

'You too, O'Leary.'

I closed my eyes and, thinking about my dream of the dead under the tarpaulins, I wondered if the discomfort of sleeping in the car would make them even harder to cover up. I wondered what problem we would have that night, and also why it was only in my sleep that that moment came back to me, and why only that moment. I'm talking about what we saw there in the days that followed, which gave us just as much sorrow, and I'm also talking about what I couldn't photograph: the evening, the prayers, the smells and the wind blowing around the scrapheap that burned night and day.

During the night O'Leary opened the car door and lay down across the front seats. I heard him tossing and turning, groaning softly. Near morning, in my dream, I was trying desperately to grab my camera, which I'd put next to O'Leary's rifle the night before, on the front seat. Then I woke up and used the flag to wipe condensation from the windows. Outside we were surrounded by mist. O'Leary was sleeping curled up on the passenger seat.

WE HAD BISCUITS and grape juice for breakfast. The sun was too low to be seen. O'Leary listened. 'The frogs are sleeping now. I'll go and sing to them.' He folded his blanket. 'What should I do with the flag?' he asked.

'Fold that too,' I said.

He shrugged. 'So there wasn't really any need for everyone to take the piss out of me yesterday at the gym. What is Montenegro, anyway?'

We were lucky. The first road we chose took us out of the forest and past fields of sunflowers that were taller and more dazzling than any I'd ever seen before. A stream ran along my side of the road. We passed a man leading a horse by the bridle. 'Stop the car! Look, there's fresh water for your flask.'

We drank from our hands. O'Leary filled his flask, then jumped over the stream and disappeared into the sunflowers. The man arrived with his horse. In an instant the sun rose above the field. The stream flowed silently. All I could hear was the sound of horseshoes on the road, like seconds ticking by. Just as the man was leading the horse past our car, O'Leary reappeared between the sunflowers and, seeing the man, cried out. O'Leary leapt over the stream and the man lowered his head and walked quickly away as if the horse were pushing him forward. The horseshoe seconds continued to tick by, gradually fading, and as if he'd been waiting for the two of us to be alone again, O'Leary pointed to the dazzling yellow sun. 'If I were you, I'd photograph that.'

I made a vague gesture with my head and said: 'So you only follow regulations every other day?' I was joking with him about the fact that he'd left his rifle in the car while he went to piss in the sunflower field.

Understanding this, he sighed with embarrassment. Then, in a light voice, seeking to make a joke of it as I had: 'The war's over.'

I shivered strangely, and in my confusion I had the impression that he had left his mother and the dunes in Lowestoft and crossed the Channel just to tell me that, here, by the stream that flowed silently at our feet.

ON A HILLTOP, a low house stood between two lime trees. A dog was sleeping in front of it. O'Leary stopped the car, turned off the engine and put on his cap. The dog looked up, but not at us. Almost as soon as we got out of the car they appeared at the door and for a moment they did nothing, then they came towards us so slowly that they looked as if they were leaving for a long time. They were both very old. The woman approached O'Leary, looked at him for a long moment, raised her hand as if she were going to stroke his cheek, and went back towards the house. Her husband stared at me with his watery old-man's eyes. The dog sighed. O'Leary was leaning against the car. The old man walked over to him, put one hand on his second-class stripes and the other hand on his own arm, presumably to tell him that he, too, had once been a second-class private. O'Leary took off his cap, just for something to do. The woman came out of the house again and called to us. Soon after that, the old man joined us in front of the door while we started drinking coffee from cups. The dog snored. The sun shone in our faces.

When I took out the camera and showed them how to stand, they didn't look very surprised. They stood close together, arms around each other's shoulders, and sniggered silently, as if mocking each other. I stepped back, took the picture and we said goodbye. O'Leary manoeuvred the car onto the road and almost immediately braked to let a lone goose waddle past.

AT THE ENTRANCE to the main road, there was a white-washed house with flowers on the windowsills. O'Leary parked near a car covered with dust. I got out and went to knock at the door. I waited, knocked again, walked to the back of the house, then retraced my steps. A woman in rubber boots was facing O'Leary. Hearing me, she turned. She was pretty, despite the dark rings around her eyes, and she looked relieved to see me. I said hello to her in German. She said hello and waited while she touched her hair with one hand and smiled an indecipherable smile. O'Leary took off his cap, put it on the steering wheel, took his rifle from the back seat, and wandered off towards the road.

The woman spoke a few words to me. I took the camera from my pocket and, counting on my fingers, pointed at the house. She shook her head. I didn't know if she was saying that she lived there alone or if she hadn't understood me. She followed me to the front door, where I counted on my fingers again. She shook her head again and her chest swelled suddenly as if she'd just been running. I showed her how to stand in front of the door. She mumbled a few words and I moved away. At that moment, O'Leary came back into the courtyard, drinking from his flask. Two young boys watched us from the roadside. I took the photograph quickly, as I'd done with the other pictures, nodded my thanks, and went back to the car. While O'Leary turned the car around so we could leave the courtyard, the woman didn't take her eyes off us. The two boys moved out of the way to let us past.

We drove along the street between the whitewashed houses and I could have knocked at other doors, but we kept going through rolling fields and at the bottom of the valleys there were windmills, a pine tree, water troughs, three more pine trees. O'Leary looked pensive as he drove and occasionally he turned to look at me.

'What do you want to know, O'Leary?'

'Nothing, sir. I just think, without a map, we'll keep going round in circles.'

I leaned down, trying to orient myself with the sun, but it was high in the sky. 'Do you remember where the sun was this morning?'

'On your side, mostly.'

'So let's keep heading north. And tell me, O'Leary, what do you do in the Signals Corps?'

40

'We lay down wiring, set up field telephones. We learn codes and when the codes change we learn the new ones.'

The road dipped and rose. In the bottoms of the valleys the windmills turned and animals drank from the troughs.

'I mean we were trained, not just once but every day, and we've laid down miles and miles of wires. I reckon if you put them all together it'd stretch from here to my house in Lowestoft, easily.'

'You could phone your mother.'

He didn't answer straight away. He started laughing quietly.

'I'd put the telephone in the dunes, where I used to sleep.'

'So you could call your mother?'

His voice quavered, full of surprise. 'Yes, sir. Exactly.'

'And what would you tell her?'

He glanced at me and almost in a whisper said: 'Quite a few things, I'm sure.'

He fell silent and looked thoughtful, then turned to me again. 'But what we say doesn't really mean anything.'

'No, O'Leary, it doesn't really mean anything.'

I started to doze. I felt the car jolting over bumps, swinging around bends, the shaft of sunlight that went from one side to the other, and in my half-sleep the woman stood before her door again, her chest rising and falling quickly.

41

'They trained us for nothing.'

I opened my eyes. 'What do you mean?'

'When we got here, it was all over. They didn't need us. I haven't shot at anybody and nobody has shot at me. I've eaten so many ration packs though . . .'

He caught up to a car with a mattress on its roof.

'I reckon I'm getting hungry, actually.'

'Stop whenever you want.'

He started looking around. When he turned to my side, there was an irritated look on his face as though the sun were bothering him. But the sun had been on his side for a while now.

'What's the matter, O'Leary?'

'Nothing, sir.'

He said nothing for a moment. His smile was very thin, but I could see it all the same.

'I won't ask you why you always take the same photographs.'

Suddenly he slowed down, turned onto a tree-lined path and stopped in front of a deep green pond.

O'LEARY WALKED BY the pond as he ate. I sat on a tree stump and watched the sky reflected in the green water until O'Leary threw a stone into it. I stood up, took a biscuit from the boot of the car and turned to the road as I ate it. I heard the stones falling into the water and invisible birds singing. O'Leary came back and put his rifle on the back seat.

'If it was evening, we could sleep here by the water.'

'It's not even close to evening. Did you see any fish?'

'Not a single one.'

'You scared them off.'

He made a noise with his mouth.

'It's the first time I've had coffee without sugar. I can still taste it.'

'What are you talking about?'

'The coffee that they gave us this morning.'

'How long can we drive with the petrol in the tank and the jerry cans?' I asked.

'Hard to know. Maybe quite a long time. But we have to think about the return journey. So it'll be half as long.'

He was smiling as he said this, but his voice was serious. We went back to the car. While he manoeuvred it onto the path, I took the roll of film out of the camera and put a new one in.

'My father had almost the same camera.'

'Almost?'

'I don't know, it's been a long time.'

I wasn't sure if he meant he hadn't seen his father in a long time or the camera. Back on the road, we used the position of the sun to keep heading more or less north.

There weren't any houses or farms now, even in the distance, but there were dozens of beehives almost everywhere you looked, poking out of the tall grass, painted lots of different colours. O'Leary kept glancing to the sides.

'Can I stop?'

He parked, got out of the car, and climbed into a field. A few yards from the first beehive, he started clapping his hands. He got closer and began yelling. He seemed to hesitate then, before running back to the car, grabbing his rifle and going into the field again. In front of the beehives, he aimed his rifle at the sky and fired. All around him, birds flew up out of the grass. O'Leary bent down, waited a moment, then returned looking half-disappointed, half-amused. 'I wanted to get rid of the taste of the coffee.'

We set off again. The road climbed. At the top of the hill, we saw the whole valley below us and, on its slopes, rooftops and long farms, cultivated fields and pine forests. At the bottom a river glimmered.

I knocked on doors until evening. I was lucky. O'Leary proved useful. His uniform had an effect. The men and the women had different reactions. The children came up to the car. The men stared intensely at O'Leary. Once the photograph had been taken, they all stayed outside their houses while we drove away. One old woman opened the door and closed it straight away, as if she'd seen the devil. I knocked again, but she didn't answer. In the house next to that, there were seven people. I had to stand all the way back by the car to fit them all in the frame. At a farm I heard noises inside, but nobody opened the door. Before the sun set, we went to wash ourselves in the river. O'Leary waded into the water up to his waist. He was thin. The water was cold and we were shivering.

We dried ourselves with blankets. We opened some ration packs. After eating, O'Leary threw one of the empty cans into the river and watched it float away. I was tired. That evening I wondered if there was any point to my idea. It was hard to think. I took out the camera to see how many pictures I had left on the film. O'Leary watched me. I handed him the camera. He turned it in his hands, put his eye to the viewfinder, and gave it back. Low in the sky, the sun dazzled us. I lay down and closed my eyes. O'Leary asked: 'Are we continuing tomorrow?'

I shrugged. 'What do you think?'

'Well, sir, if you're talking about petrol and rations, I think we can.'

'You want to sleep here? We're by the water.'

'There's nothing around. People will see us.'

The sun set. I sat up. O'Leary was sitting with his arms around his knees.

'When you slept in the dunes, everybody could see you.'

'No, nobody.'

He rested his chin on his knees.

'Do you want to know what I'd tell myself if I telephoned myself now? I mean if I was also in the dunes at Lowestoft tonight . . .'

He lifted his head and stared at the river.

'I'd tell myself: it's okay, I'm doing all right and I reckon the rations are fattening me up a bit. I'm going out in the car. I don't understand what we're doing, but I don't mind that. I'm not bored. I used the rifle for the first time since training, but the bees are deaf. And what about you? Still as skinny as ever?'

He started laughing, stood up and walked towards the water. The moon and stars illuminated him from above. I could hear the river more easily at dusk and I thought about Collins, all alone with his bedside lamp on the floor.

WE DROVE BETWEEN the riverbed and a wheat field. It was completely dark now apart from the beams of our headlights and the moon on the water. Just as O'Leary began to sing, a firework rocket rose through the sky, quite far up above the wheat. 'Stop!'

I got out of the car. I waited, and another rocket exploded, less high. It quickly died out and it occurred to me, suddenly, that the rocket had died out more quickly than the red flare that one of Collins' men had fired one evening like a prayer, lighting up the dead and the living as it fell to earth. It wasn't the same colour either. We got back in the car. 'Get your bearings and try to take us there.'

He looked ahead. 'Where, sir?'

'Where the rocket went up.'

We drove alongside the wheat field. It was immense. There were several roads. O'Leary slowed down, looked behind him, and turned onto the road to the right, which was a dead end. He stopped the car and gave me an irritated look. 'It's difficult at night.'

I waited. 'Go back the way you came.'

He made a U-turn. We found the field again. I hazarded a guess and told him where to stop.

The wheat came up to our armpits. I was hoping another rocket would go up to show us the way. O'Leary walked behind me. It was dark. The moon was too low and O'Leary muttered: 'We're going to get lost.' I turned around and he looked at me anxiously. 'Where are we going?' We set off again in a vast silence, broken only by the sound of the wheat as we brushed past it. Then we started to hear voices in the distance. We headed towards them and the singing began.

We came out of the field and jumped over an irrigation ditch. On the other side of the road, in front of the house, a fire was burning in a metal barrel. Paper lanterns hung from a tree. A dozen people were milling around, some dressed in dark suits, others in dresses. The bride, leaning against a tree, her hair crowned with flowers, reached her hand towards a paper lantern. Beside me, O'Leary wiped his forehead under his cap. 'I don't think this is a good idea.'

The singing ended. One of the figures stepped forward

and lit something. The rocket shot up but came down quickly by the roadside. The man who'd fired it walked across the courtyard, stopped in front of the rocket, and saw us. He looked very tall and very strong. He was like a giant in the night. The people near the house were watching us too now. Forcing myself to joke, I said to O'Leary: 'Don't be afraid. You won the war.'

We walked forward. O'Leary slipped his hand under the strap of his rifle. 'I didn't win anything.'

The man did not take his eyes off him. When we were standing in front of him, he shook his head and called out in a deep voice like a bear's. A young man came towards us. He was wearing a dark suit, like the giant. There was a real, pretty flower on his jacket. I realised that he was the groom. The man spoke to him in rapid German.

The groom said: 'My father asks what you want so late at night.'

His English was slow but correct. I took the camera from my pocket.

'I came to photograph you.'

The groom translated. The man stared at me while he gave his answer.

The groom said: 'He asks why you come from a field in the night to photograph us.'

I said the first thing that came to mind. It was something I'd done a long time ago in the Scilly Isles to pay for my first camera. 'It's for a census.'

'I don't understand.'

'I have to count you.'

The groom translated. The man burst out laughing. He said something to his son, stared at me for a long moment, and returned to the house.

'He said go back in the field. We know how many of us there are.'

When he had joined the others in front of the house, the man said a few words and they all started to laugh. The groom didn't move. He stayed by the roadside with us. 'Why do you want to photograph us?' he asked.

I was trembling because I was frightened.

'Follow me, O'Leary.'

The groom said in a low voice: 'Don't stay here.'

He was frightened too. I walked towards the house. I could feel the heat from the fire in the barrel. The bride moved away from the tree and went into the house with two other women. The men gathered together. I turned towards the road. O'Leary was still there, with the groom. One of the men came over, pointed at the camera in my hand, put his hand in his hair and struck a pose. The others laughed again. The paper lanterns swayed in the branches. The man with a bear's voice started to sing. The others chorused behind him and the song followed me while I walked away. When I passed the groom, he said: 'Don't go back in the field, it's too big. You'll get lost. Take the road.'

O'Leary followed me. We crossed the road and went into the wheat field.

WE DIDN'T GO back through the same field we'd come
from, so we couldn't follow the path we had made through
the wheat back to our car. The moon gave us light but
we advanced haphazardly. The sky was immense, like the
field. We couldn't hear anything. All we could see was the
wheat and the sky, stretching out into infinity. The man
with the bear's voice was still laughing in my face. I tried
to forget his song. A dozen times I imagined a company of
soldiers led by Collins emerging with me from the wheat
field. A dozen times the man with the bear's voice lowered
his eyes.

O'Leary walked beside me, a few yards away. Rifle at his
shoulder, he looked like he was going hunting.

'Why didn't you listen to me when I was calling you?'

He said nothing.

'O'Leary!'

'What could I do? I was on my own.'

His voice was plaintive. I stopped to look around. O'Leary kept walking. I called him and he came back towards me. In a soft voice, as if afraid that someone would hear us, he said: 'Do you know where we are?'

'You know perfectly well that I don't.'

'Aren't you tired?'

I didn't respond straight away.

'Do you want to sleep here?'

'No, because tomorrow nothing will have changed. We'll still be lost. But I would like to rest for a while.'

We sat down. We couldn't see each other through the wheat, but I could hear him breathing. The moon floated above us. I looked at it for so long that it grew blurred.

'Do you want to drink?'

He pulled the stalks of wheat apart and passed me the flask. I drank some water and handed it back. He took a drink too.

'So, I know I told you that, when I was in Lowestoft, I used to look at the sea because I just felt like it. But really that's not true. It wasn't only for that.'

I forced myself to ask: 'Why then?'

'I can't tell you.'

'Suit yourself.'

His voice changed. More quietly, he said: 'You can suit yourself too.'

'What, O'Leary?'

'Your photographs, I mean. You don't have to tell me what they're for.'

He lay on his back, and his voice grew even quieter. 'Maybe the car is really close.'

After a moment, I heard him move. I pulled the stalks of wheat apart. He was lying on his side, with his back to me, asleep with one hand on the rifle. I woke him up and we set off across the field. We came out on the road, a long way from the car. We could see it because the moonlight was shining on the windows. I slept on the back seat, O'Leary in the front. That night, the dead left me in peace. They didn't lift up the tarpaulins with their legs. Or maybe they did but when I woke up I couldn't remember. I spent that night standing in the wheat field watching fireworks. I can still see them. All I have to do is close my eyes. I couldn't see anything else – not the sky nor the wheat nor the earth – and I had a desperate desire to move closer. The fireworks were terrifying and beautiful. I could talk about them forever, I don't know why.

DAYLIGHT ENTERED THE car. My back was aching. I wanted to fall back asleep but O'Leary's snoring kept me awake. Suddenly he cried out, said a few incomprehensible words, and started snoring again. I got out of the car without making a sound, opened the boot and ate a breakfast of rations and fruit juice. I couldn't hear anything, not even an insect. The sky was growing lighter, but the sun had not yet appeared. In the silence I remembered the incredible fireworks of my dream, again and again, as if I were trying to memorise it. That's why I can still remember it so perfectly.

I took a few steps along the road and then came back. O'Leary was sitting up in the passenger seat. I could only see the top of his head. Through the open boot, I asked: 'Did you sleep?'

Without turning around, he said: 'No, there's this gap between the seats. I should have stuffed the blanket in there.' He rubbed his head, put on his cap, and came to join me.

Sitting on the edge of the car boot, he looked down at his shoes.

'Aren't you hungry?'

He shook his head. 'I dreamed that I'd lost my rifle.'

'If you dreamed, you must have slept.'

He looked up. 'Not necessarily.'

He drank some grape juice and we set off. The sky continued to lighten. We got lost again. The roads between the wheat fields all looked alike, but far off on the left I saw the house of the wedding, and as we passed it I spotted the groom, sitting on the doorstep, hands interlocked between his legs. We drove another hundred yards. 'Stop the car!' O'Leary braked. The car came to a stop. 'Go back over there!'

He stared at me. He, too, had recognised the house and the groom. 'Why?'

A vein was throbbing under his eye.

'Do what I tell you.'

He lowered his eyes. 'Don't you think we should just leave them in peace?'

I got out of the car and headed towards the house. O'Leary came up behind me.

'No, sir, we shouldn't go there.'

He said this timidly, in a quiet voice.

'Go back to the car. I don't need you.'

He stopped where he was. I continued alone towards the house. Since hearing us speak, the groom had not stopped staring at me.

When I entered the courtyard, he got up. He looked tired and surprised. Some smoke still rose from the barrel. The paper lanterns hung from the branches. 'Why have you come back?' I took the camera from my pocket. He smiled sadly and stared at the camera. 'I thought about it again during the night, but I still don't understand.'

My heart was beating fast and I was afraid that he would notice.

'Is this your house?'

'Yes.'

I was about to leave, but instead, looking up at a first-floor window, I said: 'Go and fetch her.'

He shook his head. 'No. Please. She's sleeping.'

I heard O'Leary come into the courtyard.

'I told you to go back to the car.'

'Sir, leave him in peace.'

I turned and yelled: 'Get out of here, O'Leary!'

He didn't move. He stared at me for a moment and lowered his eyes. I turned back to the groom. He took a step forward and said: 'I'll do it on my own.'

'No. Go and fetch her.'

He looked to the side and his lips moved. I realised that he was practising what he would say to me. Then, speaking in a loud voice, and slowly so as not to make a mistake, he said: 'If you want, I can get you something to drink and we can talk. I can get you something to eat too. But let her sleep.'

'Go and fetch her.'

He started to tremble. O'Leary muttered something behind me. I wanted to leave but the door opened and the bride appeared, a sheet around her shoulders. Her hair was mussed up. She said a few words. The groom shook his head and stared at me, his eyes filled with hate.

For a moment he looked like his father, the man with the bear's voice, then he spoke to his wife, who went back into the house. I moved forward to stop her. On the doorstep he caught my arm but I was stronger than him. I grabbed him by the throat. He struggled and O'Leary rushed towards us and tried to separate us in such a clumsy way that it was impossible to tell whose side he was on. I didn't know who I was fighting against either and suddenly we heard the bride crying through the open door. She came towards us without the sheet, dressed in a nightgown, and sobbing, she spoke to her husband, took his hand, and they turned towards me. They didn't move at all now, except for the boy's trembling body. I stepped back and photographed the two of them as soon as O'Leary moved aside.

In the silence that followed, O'Leary picked his cap off the ground, the groom looked up at the paper lanterns, his wife put her head on his shoulder, and I left the courtyard breathless with rage. I went quickly to the car, sat behind the wheel, and as I turned the key in the ignition, a vague impression that had been with me since we first set off was transformed into a certainty. For the past two days we had been driving the car belonging to Dinslaken's prosecutor, the man they were going to hang. And it was his wife, imploring the guards in her Sunday best, who had grabbed my arm outside the gymnasium. O'Leary appeared at my window, waited a moment, then walked around the car and sat in the passenger seat.

JUST BEFORE NOON I parked the car outside a café. There were a few houses on either side of the road. In the distance I could see some factory chimneys and, even further in the distance, a town. O'Leary was sleeping. Turning to wake him, I saw a scratch on his temple. I also noticed he was starting to grow a patchy beard. I closed my eyes for a moment and tried to remember what I had seen since that morning, since the valley and the newlyweds' house. Almost nothing remained, just vague images of woods, the river, a bridge. It was as if everything had closed in on itself as I was passing it.

Three men were drinking at a table. Behind the bar, a young woman and an older woman were bent over a magazine. The men looked down. The young woman stepped back and leaned against the sideboard filled with bottles. I didn't know enough words so I made a couple of gestures. The woman pointed at the table next to the one where the three men were sitting.

The light was dim because of the curtains. There was an enamel bird inside the clock. I could hear the seconds tick by. O'Leary had leaned his rifle against the table: it slipped and clattered to the floor. The young woman jumped and, while O'Leary bent over to pick it up, she lowered her eyes and started to smile. At the same time two of the three men behind me stood up and left. O'Leary put the rifle on a chair and his cap on the table, which smelled of wax and cologne. Whenever my eyes met O'Leary's, he looked away. Since the valley and the newlyweds' house, we hadn't spoken a word to each other. The woman served us a plate of cheese and slices of bread. The young woman brought us water.

O'Leary didn't eat much. His scratch had bled. I wondered who had given it to him, the groom or me. Behind me, the man, who was now alone, started speaking in a calm voice. He didn't stop, even though neither of the women paid him any notice. O'Leary looked over my shoulder and finally I realised that the man had been speaking to him. 'What's he saying?' I asked.

He waited, pretending to listen carefully, then in a quiet, serious voice, told me: 'He says his wife is cheating on him with a man who sells rabbits.' I almost choked. The man fell silent. Again we could hear the seconds. Then he stood up, walked past our table and left the café.

A murmur arose, a strange sound that I didn't recognise. O'Leary turned his head, trying to work out where it was coming from. Behind the bar, the two women looked worried. The sound was coming from the direction of the road, but we couldn't see anything through the curtains. It grew louder. Now it sounded like the distant roar of a river in flood. O'Leary grabbed his rifle and went outside. The older woman muttered something to the younger woman, and as I stood up she too went outside.

O'Leary was standing in front of me, perfectly still. To my right was the woman. The prisoners advanced along the road in the bright sunlight in almost military ranks. They seemed to be breathing as one and they never looked to the side nor even at the road but at some invisible fixed point through the back of the men ahead of them. What had sounded like a river in flood was in fact hundreds of tin plates and flasks knocking against one another and slicing through the burning air. But there was something strange, something that struck me as off, and I stood there for a while without knowing what it was, before finally noticing that the prisoners were marching without any escort and appeared to be going where they had to go by themselves. For an instant I even had the impression that O'Leary, standing there motionless with his rifle, was the only one there to lead them. Then, through the ranks of prisoners, on the other side of the road, I glimpsed clean uniforms and rifles on shoulders.

The tin racket faded. The dust settled. Beside me, the woman hadn't moved. O'Leary turned to us. He wanted to say something but the woman stepped forward into the road and stood there for more than a minute watching the prisoners march away. O'Leary shook his head and smiled strangely. The woman came back to us, glanced at O'Leary and his strange smile, went into the café, and we heard the key turn inside the lock. O'Leary looked at the café with a puzzled expression. Then he rushed over and knocked at the door.

'Come on,' I said. 'Let's just go.'

He knocked harder. We heard yells from inside. He held the rifle and was about to smash the door down with the butt when it suddenly opened, a hand appeared and threw his cap into the dust. He picked it up and, grimacing, wiped the dust off.

'If you want, I can go and fetch them.'

'Why?'

'To photograph them.'

'If you want.'

I leaned against the side of the car. I knew they wouldn't open the door. He turned back to the door and waited for a long time without moving before knocking again several times, as if this were the house of someone he knew. Then he pressed his face to the window to look inside.

'I don't see them.'

'Let's go. If they open the door, I'll have to pay for the meal.'

'You could photograph them and not pay them.'

'Come on.'

He kicked the door, gave a very loud laugh, and walked away. As he drove the car, he let his free hand sail in the wind. We looked for roads that didn't go through the town. We crossed marshes where birds stood on their long legs. He let go of the steering wheel for a second.

'Whose car is this?'

I told him what I'd thought outside the newlyweds' house: 'The Dinslaken prosecutor's. But they're going to hang him. Or they already have.'

'Why?'

'I don't know.'

He turned and stared at me.

'Keep your eyes on the road.'

We left behind the marshes and the tall birds. O'Leary had wound the window up. He was driving slowly and carefully. I closed my eyes and remembered the real river in flood. We had stopped to listen. We looked at the sky because around us nothing had changed. I asked my brother: 'What is that?'

'I don't know.'

'Is it far off?'

We ran through the grass. It started to rain. Big clouds pursued us. I fell in the wet grass. He helped me up and we started running again. He ran faster than me. The roar got louder and seemed to change.

'What is it?'

'We'll see.'

'You think it's the storm?'

We hurtled through a field and when we were standing in front of the river in flood he grabbed me by the arm and pulled me back. The water was grey and thick, as if it had been mixed with soot. The sound of stones swept along by the current was so loud that we couldn't hear each other speak. But it wasn't water or stones flowing down the slope.

What was it? The big clouds had gone past us. So what was that sound? Was it the water, the stones? It sounded like the end of the world had begun right there in the riverbed. Leaning on his shoulder, I pulled myself up and shouted into his ear: 'I can't hear anything!'

THE DOG DRAGGED itself along by its front paws. It rolled sideways on the ballast, managed to move a little further forward, then fell into the ditch. It was lying on its side and panting, mouth wide open. O'Leary repeated: 'I didn't see him, I swear I didn't.' He turned back to the railway crossing. 'He was hidden behind the wagon.' He bent over. 'He doesn't look like he's in pain.' He whispered: 'Maybe he'll be okay. I'm going to get him some water.' He ran to the car, returned with his flask, climbed down into the ditch and poured some water into his palm. Lying on its side, the dog couldn't drink. O'Leary dripped the water over its mouth, first from his hand and then from the flask. When it was empty, he said: 'Shall I get him some rations?'

'If you give him food, he'll be thirsty.'

'So what can we do?'

I started to turn back towards the car. He grabbed my arm.

'What if we took him with us?'

'And afterwards?'

'We can leave him outside a house. Why not?'

He turned to me.

'If we take him with us, I'll tell you why I slept in the dunes at Lowestoft.'

I didn't know what to say. I was worried that I'd start laughing and hurt his feelings. We set off. The road ran alongside the railway line. Outside the gatekeeper's hut, I photographed the employee on his own, arms crossed. He looked like he was smiling even though he wasn't: it was just the shape of his mouth.

I photographed three families in a village with ten houses and thousands of lupins. I had never seen so many before. It was as if, here, it rained lupin seeds instead of water. In the last house, the man was wearing an army vest. Occasionally he would smile, but his smile was indecipherable. I had seen vests like that on corpses. His wife gave us some bread that she'd just baked. The man and his children accompanied us back to the car. O'Leary drove over hundreds of lupins. The children tried to catch the seeds that burst out of their shells and flew away.

★

The smell of the bread bothered me for a while. Then I put in a new roll of film, thinking of MacGraw, who would develop these photographs at the newspaper in the evening, when office hours were over. And late in the night, as we often did, we would spread out the pictures on the floor to discuss them, and MacGraw would undoubtedly mutter 'I see' while he thought about what he was going to say. And then, in his honest way: 'I see, but what is it?' And I would maybe reply: 'I don't know, MacGraw. What do you think of it?' I put the camera in my pocket. How many days had we been on the road? I closed my eyes and again I saw the dog at the bottom of the ditch. For O'Leary it must have been the same, even with his eyes open.

Late in the afternoon, we had the sun ahead of us. The road climbed for several miles. We passed army trucks with the sun behind them, and they came dangerously close. On our other side was a sheer drop. O'Leary used his hand as a visor and drove very slowly. The truck drivers didn't care if they damaged a large, expensive German car. They didn't care if they pushed it over the edge. O'Leary parked the car while he waited for the convoy to pass. Before setting off again, I trapped the flag in the back-seat window. Soon after that, we stopped at the top of the hill. I walked to the edge of the slope. The river appeared at the bottom of a gorge, and where the sun lit it up, it was unbelievably blue. Leaving the shade of the cliff, a tiny rowing boat moved across the turquoise water. For a second I wanted to take a photograph, then I went back to the car.

The sun was going down. O'Leary watched it, motionless, on the roadside.

'Do you want to see the river down there?'

He shook his head.

'Will we go back the same way we came here?'

'I don't know.'

I thought about the turquoise water and wondered if it looked the same colour to the person inside the rowing boat.

'I should have killed it there and then.'

'It's not your fault.'

'I often used to think, when I was in the dunes, that I'd be happy if I had a dog. I wouldn't want to telephone myself right now.'

He didn't say anything else. I went back to see the river. It was completely covered by shade now and the rowing boat had disappeared.

We followed the road back down to the river and crossed

it over a metal bridge. After that the colours vanished, everything drowned in darkness, and I thought about the boat, tiny from above, and suddenly I was sitting inside it, across from the person who was rowing it, and I asked him how long he'd been on this peaceful water and I looked him in the eye, trying to figure out if he was a man or a boy and I asked him where his father and his mother were but he dipped the oars into the water and his gaze passed through me to where he was going. It wasn't a dream, it was just the darkening night and my tiredness and O'Leary's silence playing tricks on my mind. In the distance we saw the outline of a village.

THE HOUSES MUST have been lit only by candles or by oil lamps. Our headlights were brighter than all the windows put together. We stopped at a fountain and drank from our hands, then O'Leary filled his flask. After the village we didn't go far. There was a barn a hundred yards from the road. We drove towards it and the closer we got, the more habitable it looked in the headlights' beam. But when O'Leary turned them off, it suddenly appeared sinister. 'What do you think?' I asked.

'If there's hay inside, maybe . . .'

He took his rifle from the back seat and went to look. One side of the double doors was open. As we went inside, we heard something move then saw a shape rise up in the darkness. We ran back outside. The figure appeared at the door, with a misshapen hat and a grey beard, illuminated by the moon behind us. He was an old man. His eyes shone in the night. He started to speak. His voice didn't carry far but he kept talking, talking and scratching his leg. Suddenly he froze and fell silent, perhaps because he had just caught sight of O'Leary's rifle. I took the camera from my pocket. 'Turn the headlights on, O'Leary,' I said. 'Hurry up!'

There was enough hay for all of us. We had spread out our blankets and started eating the ration packs and the bread that the woman had given us. The door's hinges were broken and it couldn't be closed, so some light from the moon and the stars came in. The old man made noises in his corner. O'Leary whispered: 'I don't know if I'll be able to sleep here.'

'Why not?'

He turned his face towards the noises.

'We have nothing to fear,' I told him. 'He's older than your grandfather.'

'Maybe, but it's not him. If I go in the car, can I take the back seat?'

'Sure, but it's uncomfortable there too.'

'Better than the front, I bet.'

'Where did you sleep in Dinslaken?'

'In a school.'

He took his flask, started unscrewing the lid, and then stopped. After a moment he said: 'This is the third night.'

Finally he opened the flask and passed it to me.

★

Soon after that, the old man stood in front of us with his arms full. He kicked the straw out of the way and put a spirit stove on the concrete floor. On top of that he placed a blackened saucepan. He opened a bag, lit a match, and O'Leary and I leaned close to peer inside. There were about twenty eggs at the bottom of the bag. He lit the stove. From his pocket he took a knob of margarine, which he tossed into the saucepan. With surprising speed, he broke all the eggs into the pan and beat them with a spoon while they cooked. He turned off the stove and handed me the spoon. I shook my head. He offered it to O'Leary. 'Don't touch it,' I warned him. 'If the eggs are too old, you'll get sick. There's nothing worse.'

'If he's going to eat them, it means he knows they're good.'

'You think so? Well, do what you want.'

The old man shrugged, sat in front of us, put his hat to one side and patiently ate the twenty-egg omelette, taking care not to get food in his beard. Through the half-open door I saw a few stars. O'Leary lay on his straw bed and when the old man had finished his meal and returned to his corner, he fell asleep. I lay down but kept my eyes open. Several times the barn was illuminated by the flame of a match. I wondered if the old man was being careful, with all this hay. I waited until the darkness had lasted a while before closing my eyes and finally letting myself sleep.

That night, too, the dead pushed up with their grey legs. With Collins' men, I tried to hold the tarpaulin in place. It was impossible. Nobody had enough strength, but nobody needed help except me. I had the feeling that O'Leary was close behind me somewhere and I wondered why he didn't put down his rifle and come and help me. I wondered why, since the dead didn't want the tarp there, not one of us thought to simply give up and go home. As I woke, I accidentally rolled against O'Leary. He sat up, cried out, and then fell back asleep.

I woke once more towards morning. O'Leary was snoring beside me. Outside I could see the bonnet of the car gleaming faintly as the stars paled. I tried to go back to sleep, wondering what the photograph of the old man would look like when it was developed, seeing him again standing in the beam of the headlights, hat in one hand, the other hand making a military salute.

SUNLIGHT CAME INTO the barn. The old man was gone. The air was filled with dust. I went out and saw O'Leary a hundred yards away, by the roadside, the rifle at his shoulder, next to a man standing beside a bicycle. He returned while I was eating breakfast.

'Nice chat?' I asked.

'Yes and no. I just kept saying yes to him.'

'Maybe he kept telling you that you were an ugly bastard.'

He started laughing and went to get a can of grape juice from the boot, but there were none left. He drank water from his flask and handed it to me. Three boys came towards us. The biggest was maybe ten years old. They stopped and watched us. We folded the blankets and poured the contents of a jerry can into the car's petrol tank. The boys didn't move. When we drove onto the road, they started running towards the barn. We drove for a moment and then I turned to the back seat. 'Did you move the flag last night?'

He shook his head. 'No, sir.'

'The old man must have taken it then.'

'Is that my fault?' he asked.

I told him it wasn't.

We found the river where I'd seen the rowing boat. The water was grey because the sky had clouded over. We were going in the same direction as the current, but much faster. The sun disappeared and the water looked even slower. I couldn't stop staring at it. There was something mysterious about that water. Occasionally there was a barge washed up on the bank. O'Leary didn't speak either. He didn't slow down or turn to look at me when a house appeared, even when it was by the side of the road or looked easy to get to. He drove as if, for him too, our only aim that day was to descend the river.

The horse was lying across the road. It had been unhitched and the cart pushed onto the roadside. In front of us another car was waiting. Its driver got out and stood next to the man and the woman leaning over the horse, which was trying to lift its head. The first drops of rain fell and suddenly the sky turned dark and we were in the middle of a downpour. We could hardly even see the driver running back to the shelter of his car. The man, the woman and the horse had disappeared behind the curtain of water. O'Leary turned off the engine. We could hear nothing but the rain hammering on the car roof. O'Leary spoke over the din: 'One day it rained like this in the dunes. I'd got everything ready to spend the night there. I'd collected firewood and I had food to eat. I had my best sleeping bag. When it started raining, I thought it wouldn't last long. But then it began pouring down like this. If I'd tried to go home, I'd have got lost. I covered myself with the sleeping bag and when it was soaked through I wrung it out. I did that all night long.' He turned to face me. 'If I telephoned myself now, I'd say: do you remember that night we spent in the rain?' He started laughing, and suddenly the din faded, the light returned, and we saw the horse getting to its feet, stretching its neck and coming towards us, enormous and streaming with water.

There were lots of houses along the river. At one point, I said: 'Go on, O'Leary, I'll let you choose this time.' He whistled a few notes to express his appreciation of the importance of this task. He took his time before stopping outside one of the houses and got out first to show me he was up to it. That first photograph was a good one. There were a lot of people and none of them made a fuss. O'Leary continued to choose, sometimes luckily, sometimes less so, just like me. I took the pictures quickly and we went on our way. The sky threatened rain again. The river accompanied us more than we followed it. O'Leary stopped so often that, between houses, I almost immediately forgot the faces and the poses that I had just photographed. One family blurred into another. Except for the time when all the children were girls and the tallest one couldn't keep her eyes off O'Leary. Her mother pinched her side. She lowered her eyes. Her father was obese. Despite the overcast sky, it was a good day. O'Leary got out of the car first, and if there was no one outside he would knock at the door, wait, walk around the house, go back to the door and knock more loudly, and then leave the rest to me. Hardly anyone gave us trouble. I had to change the film and we forgot to eat. We didn't feel hungry until mid-afternoon.

THE CHURCH OVERLOOKED the river. The walls were yellow, the roof covered by wooden tiles. I pushed the door open. The vaulted ceiling had been painted with crescent moons at different moments of the year, with a star here and there among them. There was an altar carved into the stone and a bench on each side. Beneath the only window, above the altar, there was a cross. That was all there was: the altar, the cross and the benches. I went outside. O'Leary had opened the car boot and was looking through the ration packs. He said: 'There's less and less choice.' He helped himself and moved out of the way. A few drops of rain started to fall. I took my rations and went back into the church. I had just started eating when O'Leary entered, leaned his rifle against the altar, sat facing me on the other bench and opened his ration pack. We sat six feet apart. He kept glancing up at me as he ate.

'What do you want to know?'

'No, nothing.'

He forced himself to stop looking at me.

'Go ahead, O'Leary.'

'You were sleeping in the same hotel as the colonel.'

'Yes.'

'So you know him?'

'Yes.'

He waited a moment, and then: 'In the girls' school, we have camp beds. It's okay . . . but really it's not okay. I think the others don't like me.'

'Why?'

'Because I arrived after the war. Is it my fault if it was all over when I got here?'

I shrugged and asked: 'Why did you mention the colonel?'

'Almost all of the soldiers who arrived afterwards like me are sleeping in the boys' school. I'd like to sleep there too.'

'You want me to ask him?'

'Yes, sir, because I'd like to chat with everyone in the evenings in the girls' school, but I have the feeling that they'd say: shut up, O'Leary, you didn't get here till it was all over, so what do you know about it? So I watch them play cards. They let me do that. It doesn't cost them anything.'

He shook his head bitterly.

'But maybe I'd be the same if I were in their shoes. Saying shut up to the ones who got there too late . . .'

He started eating again, looking up at the crescent moons on the ceiling. Through the half-open door we heard the rain, and in a cheerful voice O'Leary said: 'Are we allowed to eat here? I bet we're not.' He leaned towards me and smiled. 'But we won, so we can eat wherever we want.' He pointed up at the ceiling. 'But I've never seen moons like that at night, in Lowestoft.'

Through the window above the altar I saw a gleam of light, then a cloud, then another gleam. The window was so small that they seemed to pass very quickly. Only now, since it was covered with dust, did I notice the replica of a flat-bottomed boat on the window ledge. O'Leary took the flask from his belt and handed it to me. There was hardly any water left. We got one mouthful each. After that, he lay down on the bench, put his hands under his head, and looked at the ceiling.

'The tallest girl, earlier . . . Did you notice how she was staring at you?'

'Yes.'

There was a bouquet of wilted wildflowers on the altar. The clouds sped past behind the small window. A gleam, a cloud, a gleam. I didn't know where we were. O'Leary had his eyes closed. I thought he was falling asleep, but he said: 'Ever since yesterday, I've had a craving for eggs.'

'We could try to find some.'

He was longer than the bench and his feet stuck over the end. He asked: 'How many did he eat that night?'

'About twenty.'

'I wonder what he'll do with the flag.'

His eyes were still closed. We had talked a little bit, but the silence quickly enveloped us.

'Are you sure that she was looking at me?'

'Yes.'

'When you see her on the photograph, will you remember?'

'I'm sure I will.'

I was half-lying. He lifted his feet onto the bench. He turned his face towards me and quickly opened his eyes as if he wanted to check that I was still there.

'In Lowestoft, I slept in the dunes because I was frightened at home. In the dunes I slept well most of the time. Except for the night when it rained.'

'What were you frightened of, at home?'

He smiled faintly. I waited, but he didn't say anything else.

'Don't fall asleep, O'Leary.'

'No, sir.'

I stood up and took a couple of steps towards the altar. Below the bouquet of wilted flowers, there was a sheet of paper folded in two. I could glimpse words on the inside. I went outside. I was thirsty. It was raining, but so little that you could have counted the drops. I held my hands like a bowl under the roof gutter and waited.

It had been raining like this, just a few drops, when we left the camp at dawn. It would have taken a year of that kind of rain to put out the scrapheap that had been burning since we arrived. I was walking past a hut when I heard someone calling: 'Come! Come!' I looked around, saw him moving, and went over to crouch in front of him. He was sitting away from the path and the huts and he smelled of smoke from the burning scrapheap. The army blanket covered his head and shoulders. How old was he? His eyes were dark and his hands were grey with ash. There was some bread beside him, and some rations. Between his knees he held a cup filled with water. His voice seemed muffled by the blanket.

'What do I look like?'

'You look fine.'

'Tell me the truth.'

'You're fine. Do you want something? Do you want me to help you stand so you can go home?'

He didn't want anything, just to talk with me.

'I'm scared. Since you got here, I've never been so scared. You understand? I can eat. They're not killing us any more. But since you've been here I have an imagination again. You understand?'

I nodded, although what I wanted to say was: yes and no. I didn't say anything. I didn't think to ask him his name. I'd only forget it again anyway. I couldn't tell from his accent what country he was from. He saw the camera in my hand.

'Come back and take my picture when I'm looking better.'

His finger traced something in the air.

'I wrote a few words on a plank. I'll try to find it again because I don't remember what it said. You can photograph the two of us – me and the plank. It's more than a plank.'

'Okay,' I lied. 'I'll photograph both of you.' In an hour he'd have forgotten me.

I would have forgotten him too. The day we left, Collins' regiment was replaced by a medical unit. We were going across Germany in the other direction and two days later we would be in Dinslaken.

I stood up. He raised his head towards me and from there his voice was no more than a murmur. 'Come back and take my picture when I'm looking better. I'll have found the plank by then.'

I nodded. He had everything he needed – bread, water, rations and a blanket – but I didn't dare walk away without saying anything. It was the last time I saw him.

'Do you need anything?'

He shrugged. He shook his head. Then: 'For now, no. But today I would really like to find the plank where I wrote those words. You'll see.'

I smiled stupidly, and so did he, but in his case it was because of his cracked lips. I pointed towards the closest hut. 'Do you want me to help you get home?'

He looked straight ahead. He wasn't listening to me any more. I waved to him and walked away. By the time we were leaving the camp, I had already almost stopped thinking about him. I looked for Collins' car among the line of trucks. Some of the drivers were revving engines and turning on headlights in the dawn gloom. I found the car but Collins wasn't there yet. I sat in the back seat, careful not to make any noise since McFee was dozing, his head resting on his arm, which was resting on the steering wheel, and I would never have given another thought to that man under his blanket, I would have forgotten him completely, if McFee had woken up then and broken the silence by speaking to me. Instead, for several long minutes, with nothing to do while I waited for Collins, I thought about the man and his plank with a few words on it. And as it wasn't raining any more and a pale sun was rising, I had one final thought for him: 'This is better – your blanket will dry out.'

THE RAIN HAD stopped. The road had dried, apart from the potholes. Each time we approached a house, we wondered if we would be able to take a photograph and buy some eggs. We only wanted to stop if we were sure of being able to do both, so if we didn't spot a henhouse we just kept going. The river was never far away. Sometimes we would lose sight of it, but not for long. The afternoon was reaching its end. The orange sunlight poured into the car on O'Leary's side. We never saw any henhouses from the road. We decided that if there were any, they must be behind the houses.

We left the road and bumped along between the sunflowers. Under the trees stood a brick house, only the lower half of which had been plastered, as if they had run out of time or plaster. As we got out of the car, I said: 'I'll take the photograph and you can ask if they have any eggs.'

He shot me an irritated look. I went to knock at the door. A boy of about twelve opened it. I heard a pleasant female voice somewhere inside. The boy answered her, then noticed O'Leary coming towards us and suddenly started crying. The woman came to the door, froze for an instant, then touched the back of the boy's neck with her hand. I didn't think to take the camera from my pocket. Behind me O'Leary waited, immobile. The boy kept sobbing. Suddenly O'Leary drew his hands up to his chest and started beating the air with his folded arms as if he wanted to fly. After a few seconds I realised that he was asking for eggs. I wanted to tell him to stop, that he should wait for me to take the photograph first. But then I saw that he was looking at the sobbing boy. It was for him alone that O'Leary was imitating a chicken with a rifle at his shoulder. The woman looked deep into my eyes. Her hand was still on the back of the boy's neck. The sobbing started to calm down and I took the camera from my pocket.

I took the photograph. The late afternoon light was dazzling on the bricks above them. I was about to leave but the woman signalled for me to wait. She whispered into the boy's ear and went back into the house. She returned with a framed photograph. She took her place next to the boy and held the photograph to her chest. I could make out nothing in the picture except a figure standing in front of a table.

The boy put his hands through his hair. The woman smiled at me and I pretended to press the button. The woman bowed her head twice and I went to the car.

O'Leary put his rifle on the back seat and sat behind the wheel.

'You forgot the eggs.'

'Did you see a henhouse?'

'No, but you should try anyway.'

'How do I ask?'

'Like you did before.'

'That was just to make him laugh.'

'Ask for water too.'

He got out of the car and went up to the woman and the boy, who were still in the same position, watching us. He flapped his folded arms again but only briefly and more shyly this time. After that, stepping closer to the house, he made some other gestures that I couldn't understand from here. The woman went into the house. He took the flask from his belt and handed it to the boy. The woman and the boy came back at the same time. She handed him two eggs and the boy gave him the flask, which O'Leary tried to put back in his belt. But as he couldn't manage with only one hand, the woman did it for him. He returned to the car and, while he was putting the eggs on the back seat, he said: 'I've got matches. If we empty two ration cans, we can cook them.'

We bumped along in the other direction, back towards the road. We drove for a while, the evening following us. We stopped next to a field to cut some dry grass, and while the eggs cooked in the ration cans balanced between two stones, I felt my throat tighten. What was it? The smell of the smoke and the cooking eggs? The evening air and the folded piece of paper below the wilted flowers? I was starting to drift away. So where was it coming from? From my idea for the photographs, which was slipping between my fingers like sand? Then I heard: 'They're cooked.' I went into the grassy field. My throat still felt tight. I stumbled over a tree stump. Sitting on it, I put my head in my hands, closed my eyes and began to drift far away from here, from these roads and these houses with half-whitened facades and these fields of sunflowers.

But I heard footsteps. O'Leary came over and handed me a still-warm, blackened can.

'You should eat it. It's not good cold.'

I ate the egg with my fingers. It wasn't good hot either. It tasted like the rations that had been in the can. Above us, the first stars appeared. The sunset had faded to darkness. O'Leary said: 'We need to be careful with the rations. We need about ten a day, and a couple of eggs isn't going to help. If it goes on like this, we'll be hungry.'

I threw the can away and wiped my fingers in the grass. I waited for O'Leary to go back to the car so that I could close my eyes and drift far away from here. He seemed to be sniffing the evening air. He lifted up his cap and rubbed his head. Then he crouched down, tore up a few grass stems and started throwing them like javelins. While he did this, he sang a song under his breath, as if I wasn't there, and when he'd used up all the javelins he said: 'Your photographs aren't interesting and we'll be hungry soon, but I'm better off here than waiting around in the gymnasium.'

He tore up some more grass stems and said: 'Will you take my photograph?'

'If you want.'

He nodded.

'Will that one be interesting?' I asked.

He turned to me and smiled. 'Yes, sir.'

Throwing another javelin, he asked: 'Was the egg good?'

'No.'

'Yeah, mine neither. I'd have washed the cans if I'd had enough water.'

Car headlights lit up the edge of the field and then moved away. Somewhere in the distance, a voice called out.

The silence and the darkness settled over us again, and for a long time O'Leary crouched there, looking dreamily at the sky and the field and throwing his javelins. When they were all gone, he said: 'Why are you taking those photographs?'

I remained silent. He didn't ask again. The question hadn't been for me. It had been neither whispered nor spoken out loud. It was more like a breath of wind, escaped from wild and distant winds, that barely brushed past us before continuing on its way across the field.

He turned his head. We were starting to hear something but we couldn't see anything in the darkness. It came closer, stopped, and we heard it again. O'Leary didn't move. The wild boar burst from the darkness, advanced, and stopped a dozen yards away, its huge head lifted towards us. For a minute it stayed like that, as if it had been blinded and was trying to see us.

'What do I do?'

His voice was trembling, and so was mine.

'Shut up. Don't move.'

We heard it breathing. Those breaths were more terrifying than its enormous grey head, which leaned forward suddenly. The boar began digging in the earth with its snout, groaning and grunting.

O'Leary, still crouched in the same position, whispered: 'What do we do?'

The boar raised its head, seemed to shake itself and started digging again. O'Leary reached out with one hand to the strap of his rifle and began to slide it down his arm.

'Stop, O'Leary.'

He obeyed me and stared at me, mouth open. The boar kept digging and edging closer. I could make out its eyes now. I wanted to stand up and run to the car. O'Leary was still staring at me as if awaiting a signal. Suddenly, without either of us moving, the boar groaned, raised its head and ran back in the direction it had come from. When the thunder of its retreat had faded to silence, O'Leary stood up, shouldered his rifle, gave an inhuman roar and aimed randomly into the sky. The sound of the gunshot drowned out his voice.

TURNED TOWARDS THE place where the boar had disappeared, O'Leary stood completely still. The silence returned. He seemed to be waiting to hear the echo of his yell or the gunshot. The rifle hung loosely from his hand. I could hear my heart pounding. I got to my feet. He picked up his cap, which had fallen when he shouldered the rifle, and we walked back to the car. 'Did you smell that thing? It stank like it'd been dead for a week!' He put his rifle on the back seat and we set off.

As far as we could see in the beam of the headlights, the landscape was flat and desolate, and beyond that in the night nothing stood out. In the fields the grass wasn't tall enough for us to park the car without being seen from the road. But we found the river again – it was flowing past on my side, wide and grey – and soon we saw lights in the distance, on the other side of the river, dozens of pale lights, bunched close together as if a whole town were preparing for the night. O'Leary looked at them too. 'What do we do?' A moment later, huts and warehouses appeared along the riverbank. Then a crane loomed into view, and another, and we saw pontoons and enormous piles of sand. O'Leary drove slowly. I pointed out a gravel path that led down to the riverbank. He took it and stopped at the foot of one of those piles of sand.

Even standing at its edge, you had to listen closely to hear the murmur of the river. The pale lights floated far off in the darkness. O'Leary went back to the car. I walked over to two barges that had been roped together. Each one was about a hundred feet long and so loaded with sand that their decks were level with the surface of the water. Their stems were pointing downstream. Grass and wildflowers had grown in the sand. I heard a sound, clearer than the murmur of the river, as if there were a stream or a waterfall somewhere nearby. I climbed onto the first barge and walked across to the other side. Between the two hulls there was a shrinking gap. The current rushed into it, speeding up and passing over a dam of tree trunks and branches, causing a small waterfall – nothing more than a trickle, really, but it was noisier than the river. Just as I realised I was looking at an arm and a hand emerging from the branches, O'Leary

– whom I hadn't heard coming up behind me – bent down to examine them too. 'What is it? What do you see?'

I said nothing. I listened to the clear sound of the water going over the driftwood dam and I imagined that the arm and the man were part of it too, that the miniature waterfall would not have existed without them. Leaning down beside me, O'Leary tried to see through the darkness between the two hulls. I wanted to photograph the sound of the waterfall, just like with the woman in soldier's boots in Dinslaken who was talking to herself. This time, though, it wasn't the beer playing tricks on me. 'Come on, O'Leary.'

I walked back across the barge, and as I jumped onto the dock, I heard: 'Sir, there's a dead body in the water.' His voice took a long time to reach me. He was still leaning towards the waterfall. He stood straight and turned to face me. 'Did you see it? What should we do?'

'Nothing,' I replied. 'Come on.'

I went back to the car. I heard him jump onto the dock and walk closer. I opened the boot and rummaged through the ration packs for a carton of fruit juice that we might have forgotten.

O'Leary came very close to me. 'We can't sleep here.'

His voice wobbled.

I said: 'It's late. I'm tired. So are you.'

He opened his arms. 'Yeah, I'm tired but I can't sleep here, next to it. Let's go. I'll drive, you can rest. You can sleep while I look for a better place.'

I said nothing. He smiled sadly and behind him I saw the pale lights going out one by one. I put all the ration packs into the crate. Occasionally we could hear sand pouring down the mountain behind us.

We had to start with the smallest bits of wood in the dam. They were holding back all the others, as if they'd been tied in knots. We each lay on the side of a barge and tossed the wood behind us. O'Leary had stripped off to the waist. Now, closer to the water, I could see the uniform sleeve that covered the arm. It was the sleeve of a winter coat. Sometimes the arm moved, and the hand seemed to point in a certain direction. After a while it sank, vanishing under the surface of the water with the hand, and when it bobbed up again O'Leary moaned. The bigger pieces of driftwood were harder to take out of the water. We had to kneel down and brace ourselves then pull with all our strength. But I had the impression that the dam would not give way, that it was held together by something more powerful than us, something we couldn't see from the surface, and that it wouldn't let the corpse drift downriver without a fight. O'Leary frantically pulled the big pieces of wood out of the water. He threw them behind him and started again. And suddenly the whole arm emerged, the head appeared, and the torso lifted out of the water as if something at the bottom of the river had pushed it up before letting go. The corpse fell back on its stomach. It floated in the same place for a moment and almost flipped over, but thankfully the current dragged it slowly between the two hulls, taking the rest of the wood with it. Then it passed between the stems, drifted into the distance at the same speed as the river, and soon disappeared. O'Leary sat on the sand on his barge and hung his head. I stepped over the current, silent now, to the other barge. And, seeing the rifle leaning against the sand, surrounded by the driftwood that he had pulled from the water, I said: 'Don't forget your rifle, O'Leary.'

He shook his head. 'No, sir.'

Leaning against the side of the car, I listened to the slow murmur of the river. I saw the water, darker than the night, and O'Leary's thin white back as he sat on the sand in the barge, among the grass, the wildflowers and the driftwood, and as if he were sitting next to him or in his place, I suddenly thought about McFee, Collins' driver, half-Jewish on his mother's side, who wasn't afraid of driving in the rain even when it was falling like the sea, and in my confusion and my tiredness I saw him waving regally to the river and the last few pale lights. 'Hello, hello, hello, I am the king.' And if that really had been McFee sitting on the barge, I'd have gone to sit next to him and I'd have whispered: 'You don't know what you saw there either, McFee, but don't worry about it and live a long, long life. And tonight, you can be the king of the sky and the pale lights, and when the rain falls like the sea in your hometown, drive carefully, and when night comes, sleep, McFee, sleep, listen to the rain and try to have sweet dreams. Sleep and think no longer of the terrifying nights.'

I listened to the river, I thought about McFee, and again I felt my throat tighten. It hurt. There was a stone inside it, rising and falling. The corpse that we'd set free had not changed anything. And this pain in my throat, I was sharing it with McFee. I didn't know why. I looked up and saw the only constellation in the sky that I knew. Then on the barge O'Leary stood up, looked around for a moment, and bent down to pick up his rifle and his shirt.

Back on the dock, he turned to face the river for a brief moment then came and leaned against the car beside me.

He put down his rifle and put on his shirt. I pointed to the sky in front of us. 'Look at those stars. They're in the shape of a house. You see it?'

'A house? No.'

'It's leaning. With three little stars across the middle. You see them?'

'No.'

I took his hand and pointed to the constellation.

'There, O'Leary. Try to look.'

'Well, it's easy when you know where it is.'

'Look! A leaning house with three stars inside it.'

'I don't see anything.'

His voice was low and indifferent. He withdrew his hand, picked up his rifle and put it in the boot. Well, I hadn't tried very hard to show him either. He went to sit by the pile of sand, rested his chin in one hand and looked up as if he were searching for the three little stars in the constellation. But he probably wasn't. He was probably just looking at nothing in particular.

LYING ACROSS THE front seats, O'Leary didn't move. Occasionally he coughed, as quietly as he could. He breathed slowly. I closed my eyes and felt vaguely ashamed at having talked to McFee, at having let myself go like that. But I didn't regret it. Each time I moved I felt, in my shirt pocket, the three rolls of film I had taken since Dinslaken pressing against my chest. That way, I knew how many families I had photographed. I started counting the ones I still remembered. I wanted to know how many I had already forgotten. The result didn't matter. It was just a way to pass the time while I waited to fall asleep.

I was close to the end of the families from the first day when O'Leary's low voice interrupted me: 'Can I roll down the window?'

From the sound of his voice, I could tell that he too was lying on his back.

'Go ahead. Half open.'

He sat up, lowered the window, and lay down again. I'd lost track of my calculations.

'Did you stuff your blanket in the gap between the seats?'

'Oh, yeah!'

I heard him making small movements. He must have been folding and unfolding his long legs.

'What scared you?' I asked.

'It's the first dead body I've ever seen.'

'No, not tonight. Back home in Lowestoft. What were you scared of?'

A long silence ensued, so long that I thought he must have fallen asleep.

'I don't want to talk about it. Not now.'

'Suit yourself.'

He moved, probably onto his side.

'Would I gain anything by talking about it?'

'I don't know. Probably not.'

I waited, and as he was silent I decided to start my calculations again at the beginning. But then he asked: 'Will it go all the way to the sea?'

It took me a few seconds to understand.

'I don't know. It depends. I don't know how far it is.'

'If it's a long way, maybe something will stop it before then.'

'Probably.'

'And then?'

'I don't know that either. Maybe we'll find it and fish it out.'

'It's all alone in the water. I find it hard to understand.'

'Don't worry about it.'

He breathed slowly and I was sure that his eyes were open.

'I've always been a bit afraid of the water.'

'Try to sleep.'

And in a hoarse voice: 'And if it does go all the way to the sea, what then?'

He said this so quietly that I knew the question wasn't addressed to me. Next, I heard him tossing and turning, and after a while I saw his hand gripping the headrest of the seat. Then he seemed to calm down.

'Goodnight.'

'You too, O'Leary.'

Not long after that, some sand trickled down the pile outside, breaking the silence.

'What's that?' he whispered.

'It's sand.'

I closed my eyes. How long had they been closed? I could barely hear O'Leary breathing behind the seats. I could have sworn he was asleep.

'You think it drifted downriver?'

'You saw it too, didn't you?'

'Yes, but not for long. And not in the middle.'

'What difference does that make?'

'Maybe it turned towards the shore and got trapped somewhere. Maybe it's not far away from us now. I want to go and see.'

'And then what?'

'I'll send it back downriver.'

'It's still going downriver now. Everything goes into the middle of the river, because that's where the current is fastest.'

'No, sir, I think the opposite is true. The current pushes everything towards the shore. And I won't be able to sleep if it's still there.'

'It's not there.'

'I want to make sure.'

He opened the door and got out. I waited, and then got out too. He was putting on his shoes. He stood up and we exchanged a glance. He looked dejected. His lips moved. He wanted to say something. But instead he went to the car boot to fetch his rifle, and when he came back and stood in front of me I said: 'Stay here. I'm sure the current has taken it.'

He shrugged, to show his doubt, then in a painful voice said: 'I'm a telephonist, sir.'

'What? What are you talking about? What difference does it make if you're a telephonist or not?'

He shook his head without looking at me and began to walk towards the riverbank, rifle in hand. When the darkness had hidden him from me, I called out: 'How will you put it back in the water if you find it? You're all alone and you don't have any tools!'

He didn't answer.

In a louder voice, I yelled: 'Go all the way to the sea if you want, O'Leary, but don't call for me! O'Leary, you hear me? Don't call for me and don't come back to fetch me!'

I waited, facing downstream, listening out for any sound. I did this for quite a long time, then went back to sleep in the car. I was thirsty, but he'd taken the flask with him.

All night long, my mouth was parched. In my dream I wanted to get up and drink water from the river, but it was muddy. So I wanted to cross it and climb towards the pale lights to ask for something to drink, but the current was too strong. And sometimes O'Leary would hand me the flask but I didn't dare drink that water either, as if it had been poisoned. All night long my thirst tormented me, but it saved me from the dead and their grey legs.

THE FIRST GLIMMERS of daylight woke me. I wasn't thirsty any more and one by one my dreams came back to me. The sun had not yet risen, but already the river was less dark. I got out of the car without making a sound and, going around to open the boot, I saw O'Leary lying on his back at the foot of the mountain of sand. He had dug a hole and slept deep inside it. The sand was almost the same colour as his uniform. Trickling down all night long, it had filled the spaces around him. The rifle was planted next to him, barrel buried in the sand. I chose the least worst of the ration packs, but I'd hardly started eating when I felt the same terrible thirst I'd felt earlier that night. I took the flask from O'Leary's belt and while I was drinking I heard a car go past on the road and a bird singing on the riverbank.

I finished eating breakfast and went to have a wash behind the bows of the barges so weighed down by sand that they looked as if they were sitting at the bottom of the river. A tree with green leaves floated past. In the place where the pale lights had shone the night before, there was a green and mauve hill, and after a while I saw a house, then another. They were camouflaged by the vegetation and only became visible when I stared at them. There were more than a dozen like that, half-hidden behind the trees. There was still hardly any daylight but the bird kept singing. I couldn't tell where it was. Swallows flew over the field on the other side of the river, apparently coming from the hill and the peaceful houses, from which threads of smoke now rose, mingling together and forming a cloud in the dark blue sky above the houses. It seemed like a good place to live even early in the morning and they probably fired rockets of every colour into the sky there when people got married. Suddenly I looked down at the dark water of the river and started nodding, overcome with a sadness that I rarely felt at this hour of the day.

When I looked up again, the tree with the green leaves had continued its journey downriver. It was so far away now that it seemed to have stopped in the middle of the current, like a small island. The invisible bird did not stop singing for a single second. The sky promised a beautiful day. The river flowed on, growing lighter and lighter, and despite the brightening daylight a crescent moon remained there between the river and the houses. I decided I would go to those houses that morning to take my last photographs and then return to Dinslaken.

I heard footsteps behind me.

'Do you remember whether we passed a bridge that would take us to the other side of the river?'

'Yesterday?'

'Yes.'

He crouched down, dipped his hands in the water and shook his head.

'Try to remember.'

'I'd like to, but I need to eat and we have hardly any food left.'

He looked up at the sky.

'We did cross one, I remember now, but I think it's a long way. Did we see another one afterwards? That I don't remember. Why?'

I didn't answer. He splashed water on his face and the top of his head and stood up, shivering.

'Did you find it?' I asked.

To start with he didn't understand what I was talking about. Then he shook his head.

'Did you go far?'

'No. I couldn't see anything. If I'd had a lamp, I'd have gone further.'

He looked at the river for a while. Without taking his eyes from it, he said: 'You think it'll go all the way to the sea?'

'I don't know. I have no idea where it is.'

I stood up.

'Go and eat, O'Leary.'

Without thinking he began a military salute, but stopped himself before his hand had touched his temple. He shrugged, smiling, and walked off towards the car. Behind the hill, the sky was yellowing. The invisible bird had fallen silent. Now I thought I could hear a human song, but it was just the slow murmur of the river. O'Leary stopped before he reached the car and turned to face me.

'I think I lost the flask last night. I don't know how it happened.'

'No, I took it earlier. It's in the boot.'

'Is there any water left?'

'A bit.'

'We'll die of thirst soon too.'

Standing by the river, I tried to remember the bridge we had crossed yesterday and wondered whether it would be better to keep going along the road and find another one. I turned to the car.

'You're the driver, O'Leary. Tell me how far the bridge was that we crossed yesterday.'

Sitting on the edge of the car boot, he opened a ration pack and stuffed some in his mouth. Then he said while eating: 'We saw lots of things yesterday, sir, and I can't remember them all, but in my opinion the bridge is a long way off and I don't think we saw another one afterwards.'

He threw away the can, and while he was drinking from the flask I joined him by the car. He showed me the hole that he'd made in the sand, which was slowly filling up.

'I dreamed about a dog. We were happy but he didn't listen to me. He was always at least a hundred yards away. I could see him in the distance. I didn't know what he looked like really but we were happy.'

I pointed at the hill. 'Find a way to get there, O'Leary. After that, we'll head back.'

'Today?'

'Yes.'

He stood there for an instant looking thoughtful, and then, trying to sound serious, he said: 'If I'd been in the engineers, I'd have made you a raft.' He looked at the hill then, and added in a low voice: 'Why? What's there?'

A light breeze enveloped us, and the grass and wildflowers that had grown in the sand on the barges bowed down. The bird started singing again. O'Leary grabbed his rifle from the pile of sand and we left.

THE CRESCENT MOON followed us long after the sun had risen. We didn't lose the river, but the hill and the houses were far behind us. We saw the piers and cables of a bridge but when we got there, we found a chain blocking the entrance. We could see the river rushing past through a gaping hole in the deck of the bridge. Around it, jagged steel and wood girders pointed up at the sky. O'Leary whistled. We waited without moving for a while, as if something might change. Finally I opened my door.

'Go and park the car. And don't forget your rifle.'

'Park it? Why?'

I gestured to the other side of the river.

'We can make it across on foot. It's solid enough. We can walk up to the hill and the houses.'

'It'll take us a while. It's a long way. We'll be hungry.'

He shook his head but didn't dare meet my eye. As I was about to get out of the car, he said: 'We can find as many houses as we want in the car. Why bother walking for hours?'

I fixed him with a hard stare.

'Do what I tell you, O'Leary. And if you want to eat, take some rations.'

I got out, and while I approached the edge of the hole, he went to park the car. We crossed the bridge. On the other side, he stayed behind me. His footsteps sounded light, as if he were walking on tiptoes. When I turned around, he was a hundred yards behind. I signalled for him to run. He paid no attention. I yelled at him angrily, and when we started walking up the hill side by side, he muttered: 'What's up with you?'

'What?'

I started laughing.

'Never mind what's up with me, O'Leary. Just stay beside me, and if a car goes past, flag it down.'

I thought that was the end of it, but after a while he said quietly: 'I've stayed beside you since we left Dinslaken. I never forget it. And last night I slept in the sand so I wouldn't wake you.'

'What's your point?'

'Nothing, that's it.'

He shifted the rifle to his other shoulder. When he next spoke, his voice was so quiet that it was almost as if he were just thinking the words.

'We're not eating well any more. Soon we'll be hungry. And thirsty. I'm going where you want for your photographs, and I think I'm doing a good job, so don't laugh at me.'

I wanted to tell him that I didn't know what I was laughing about. I wanted to tell him that sleeping in the sand had perhaps reminded him of his dunes in Lowestoft. The road was a few yards above the river. Sometimes it deviated and we lost sight of it, but we always found it again fairly quickly. The current was coming towards us and at times I felt bad for O'Leary, alone beside me. A long way behind us, the sky grew overcast. I wondered how many days it had been since we left.

'Why didn't you take any rations, O'Leary?'

'The ones that are left are inedible.'

To give myself something to do, I started watching the upper part of the river, trying to spot the tree with green leaves that we'd seen that morning as it floated towards us. Or sometimes my mind arrived before our bodies at the green and mauve hill. It drifted from house to house.

For an hour, we didn't see anyone. All we saw were some cows and a horse in a field. Once again the road moved away from the river and we lost sight of it for almost half an hour. O'Leary kept turning around to look at the sky where it was clouding over. The wind blew and then died down again. A car appeared from the bend behind us. I signalled to the driver to stop. He slowed down, but when he was close enough to see O'Leary's uniform he swerved around us and accelerated away. O'Leary stared dreamily at the car until it had disappeared. Then he turned and looked back at the clouds that were pursuing us.

'They're coming from the sea. I think we should go back to the car.'

'How do you know they're coming from the sea?'

He shrugged.

'I used to see them coming when I was in the dunes. I recognise them. It can't be far away.'

'All right, maybe so, but we're going to keep going, and the next car you see, I want you to show them your rifle.'

He stared at me without moving.

'Hold it in your hands!'

He took it off his shoulder and let it hang from his right hand. Without looking at me, he said: 'An hour from now it'll be raining and we'll still be miles away from the hill. If we keep going, I'm afraid we won't have time to get back to the car.'

'What aren't you afraid of, O'Leary?'

He shook his head and lowered his eyes. I walked a hundred yards and turned around. He'd hung the rifle over his shoulder again and was walking listlessly in the middle of the road, staring at nothing.

FOR OVER AN hour there was the most spectacular storm I had ever seen and not a drop of rain. At the first flash of lightning we ran to a corrugated iron barn, half-filled with rotting hay. The clouds were getting darker all the time, and soon they were so low in the sky that it looked like night-time. The horizon had vanished. The river flowed past, as black as the clouds. The thunder split the sky in two and the lightning was so dazzling that for a few seconds afterwards we were blinded. O'Leary sat in a corner, balancing his rifle on his knees. I sat facing him. We jumped at every bolt of lightning and didn't dare close our eyes while we waited for the thunder to follow. When the noise had died down, he licked his lips and stared into space. I waited for the first drops of rain to hit our roof. I wondered how I could catch them in the flask. I was also afraid of lightning striking the corrugated iron. O'Leary still hadn't said a word.

★

After one flash of lightning, he said: 'It's the sea, I'm sure of it. But which one?'

I waited for the roar of thunder to end.

'The Baltic, no?'

'You think?'

We were thinking about this when a boy of about twelve suddenly appeared from one side of the barn and ran past us. He was carrying a bucket in each hand and he crossed the road, ran down to the river, quickly filled his buckets then came back the way he'd gone, running past without noticing us. There was another flash of lightning, and by the time I got up and went outside to see where he'd gone, he had vanished. Not long after that, the rain started. It fell so hard on the iron roof that it drowned out the sound of the thunder. Streams started to form on the floor of the barn, criss-crossing it like veins, seeking a better path, carrying along little rafts of hay.

The tumult didn't end, and the lightning flashes gave O'Leary's face an illusory mask of anger. For a very long hour, I watched the streams make their way across the dried earth of the barn floor. Suddenly the idea of returning to the car after the storm and driving back to Dinslaken started to form in my mind, and I sighed as I dreamed of shores swept by white clouds and woke a few seconds later with a feeling of immense loneliness that nothing could fill and that made my heart beat furiously. Water was pooling on the floor now, forming new streams that I watched until the storm was over.

The rain died down and the light returned. The horizon was visible once again. We could still hear thunder but it was a little more distant each time, moving away in a direction that I couldn't calculate. Between the fleeing dark clouds, we saw little pink ones. We heard the last drops of rain on the roof and just as I stood up the boy reappeared, crossing the road and running down to the river with his buckets. O'Leary went outside and looked up at the sky. Just then, the boy saw us as he was coming back from the river, and he straightened up as if the buckets had become less heavy. When he was close enough to recognise O'Leary's uniform, fear made him burst out laughing for an instant, then as he passed us he blushed.

I said to O'Leary: 'Come on, let's get something to drink and take one last photograph.'

He seemed to hesitate, opening his mouth to speak, but then he went to fetch his rifle. Hearing us behind him, the boy turned around, stumbled, and spilled water as he regained his balance. When O'Leary told him that everything was all right and we weren't going to eat him, he lowered his head. Like O'Leary, his hair had been shaved.

We walked under pine trees. The forest grew closer, the path narrower. O'Leary walked behind me. Heavy raindrops were still falling from the branches above us. Birds were singing in the treetops. When we arrived at the clearing, it was like entering a brightly lit room. In the centre there was a low house, its facade clad with freshly sawed planks. The boy headed left towards a cistern made from welded steel plates and emptied his buckets into it. Then he went to the house, turning his face so he couldn't see us and leaving his buckets on the doorstep before going inside. As we approached, a man appeared at the door, dressed in a large shirt and a large pair of trousers. The sleeves of his shirt were rolled up to his shoulders. He was not a large man. His neck and his arm muscles were tensed. He stared at O'Leary. The boy came to the door and the man spoke to him. The boy picked up his buckets and, before he could leave, I took the camera from my pocket, showed it to him, pointed inside the house and counted on my fingers. The man came over to us and reached out his hand to take the camera. I hesitated, then gave it to him. He turned it in his hands, looked through the viewfinder and gave it back to me. Then, laughing, he signalled that O'Leary should hand him his gun. O'Leary laughed too. A woman holding a baby in her arms appeared at the door. I raised the camera to show them my intention of photographing them together in front of their house and the man immediately shook his head, laughing again. Then, as I was repeating my gestures, he touched my shoulder and, pointing at the steel cistern where the boy had emptied his buckets, pretended to take a photograph. From the serious look on his face, I realised that he wanted to show me something that he thought was worth photographing. So, again, I showed him where to stand in front of the house and, with a gesture, agreed that, when the picture had been taken, he could show me the cistern.

I took the photograph. The boy stood between his mother and father. She put her hand on the baby's head just after I'd pressed the button. With a broad, joyless smile, the man signalled to O'Leary to stand next to him for another photograph. O'Leary didn't move, so the man pretended to have a rifle in his hands and aimed it above our heads. Then he signalled that we should follow him to the cistern.

MORE THAN A dozen carp, each one weighing several pounds, were swimming around in three feet of water, and whenever they approached the surface the sunlight shone on their green scales. O'Leary watched them, fascinated. The boy went back towards the forest with his buckets. The man started talking. I stopped him with a gesture and made clear that we didn't understand. He shrugged and kept on talking. I walked around the cistern and pretended to take a photograph. After a while the man fell silent and caressed the surface of the water with both hands without frightening the carp, which kept swimming round and round without changing course, as though it was they that the hands were caressing. I said to O'Leary: 'Go and fill up your flask.'

He started walking away, and without turning around he asked: 'You think they have eggs? I'm hungry too.'

We sat on the grass between the cistern and the house. The woman brought over a plate of bread, cheese and some kind of salami. The man knelt on one knee and observed us. With a gesture he asked O'Leary to hand him his cap. The boy came back from the river and emptied his buckets into the cistern, then crouched down next to his father, who turned O'Leary's cap in his hands. There was a tattoo on his arm, no larger than a coin. I couldn't tell what the design was. He gave the cap back to O'Leary and examined him for a long moment with his pale eyes, as if trying to work out where he'd seen him before. While he examined O'Leary, he talked to himself very quietly. The boy leaned in to hear what his father was saying. We heard the baby crying in the house and the mother's voice soothing it. Then the man pointed at O'Leary and spoke to him in a mysterious voice. He was obviously asking him something. With a smile, O'Leary replied: 'Lowestoft, by the sea.'

Then, in a more serious voice: 'In the Signals Corps.'

The man opened his eyes very wide, as if they might help understand this foreign language.

'Yes, sir, we lay down miles and miles of wire, we set up field telephones and we learn codes. The codes change all the time, but it's not too complicated.'

The man continued to stare at him wide-eyed. Still looking serious, O'Leary raised an imaginary field telephone to his ear and began speaking incomprehensible sentences punctuated by even more bizarre code words. At the same time, inside the house the baby was crying, the woman's voice was soothing, and the man, imitating O'Leary, also raised a heavy field telephone to his ear and started laughing into it loud enough to drown out the cries of the baby and the mother's voice. O'Leary turned to me and then back to the man, and into his own telephone he started laughing equally loud. This went on for about ten seconds. They laughed like madmen, while staring at each other, and then stopped at the same time, both of them breathless and flushed with anger. In the silence that followed, we heard the baby crying again, the mother starting to sing, until suddenly the air was humming, everything vibrating. The sky clouded over with about a hundred aeroplanes flying so close to one another that they looked like a single giant machine. The boy shaded his eyes with his hand to watch them. But already the planes were moving away and the sky above the clearing was calm again. O'Leary and I had finished the bread, cheese and salami, and it had all been better than the best of the rations and we weren't hungry any more. The flask was filled with cool water and we could have left at that moment.

A light breeze brought us the scent of honeysuckle and suddenly I was overcome by loneliness, just as I had been in the barn. It was a loneliness without beginning or end. It was probably because of the beauty of the clearing, the fading light and the distant roar of the planes. Still kneeling on the ground opposite us, the man reached out with his hand to O'Leary's rifle, which was lying in the grass between us. He smiled, showing all his teeth, and the muscles in his forearm twitched with impatience, and I wanted to lie down for a while and close my eyes on that unfathomable sadness, so I said to O'Leary: 'Take out the magazine and the bullet in the breech and give it to him.'

'Are you sure?'

'Yes.'

O'Leary took out the magazine and the bullet and handed the rifle to the man, who held it horizontally, the barrel in one hand and the butt in the other and started speaking, apparently to the rifle itself. Then he raised the barrel and aimed at different parts of the sky. He offered it to the boy, who immediately jumped up and ran over to the buckets, grabbing them and heading towards the forest while his father handed the rifle back to O'Leary. So I lay in the grass and buried my eyes in my arms.

I SLEPT WITH the scent of honeysuckle, waking sometimes when the baby cried and falling back asleep when the mother's voice calmed it. When I finally sat up, the sun was setting behind the pine trees. I stayed sitting there, trying to work out whether my sadness had vanished with the daylight or whether it was still lurking inside my chest, ready to return at any moment. O'Leary and the boy were walking side by side near the pine trees. I couldn't hear the baby any more, nor its mother, and from here the house seemed empty. When O'Leary and the boy, continuing their walk alongside the pine forest, left my field of vision, I was alone in the middle of the clearing. The sun, setting behind the trees, seemed to burn them up, without any smoke or flames.

O'Leary and the boy eventually reappeared to my right, finishing their tour of the clearing. When he saw that I was awake, O'Leary headed towards me, the boy beside him. Standing close to me, the boy looked up with a mysterious expression at O'Leary, clearly waiting for something. O'Leary swayed on his legs and said as if he were performing in a play: 'Evening is falling, sir, as you can see.'

'Why are you talking like that, O'Leary?'

He blushed slightly.

'I just meant that it's late and that it'll take us at least two hours to get back to the car. It'll be dark by the time we get there and we'll be hungry and we won't sleep well. So . . . why don't we stay here?'

The boy looked down and smiled shyly. He knew what O'Leary was asking me. The sun was setting quickly behind the pines. Above the clearing the sky was pure and violet like a flower.

O'Leary said: 'They showed me where we could sleep. In the attic, on mattresses. It'd make a change, eh?'

The boy turned to look at me. I waited. I didn't know if I had the courage to walk back to the car and spend another night sleeping on the back seat. 'Why not?' I said.

At that moment, the woman appeared on the doorstep.

I can still see her lips smiling at me. I can still remember the scent of gardenia that seemed to emanate from the folds of her dress. She handed me a hot cup that steamed and smelled good. Sitting in the warm grass, I watched her walk back towards the house. Just then, O'Leary and the boy left the clearing with the buckets and when they disappeared into the path between the pines, the sun went out as if someone had blown on it. Again, there was nobody around me. I can still see the pine trees in the evening light and I can still smell the honey-coloured steam rising from the cup. In the house the baby was crying, the woman was singing, and I lowered my head and opened my mouth wide as if I were going to talk to the grass, but I remained silent and disoriented.

THE BOY WENT all over the place, carrying this and that. He went into the house and came out again. O'Leary and I watched him, sitting on a bench made from two logs and a plank. When he walked past us, the boy gave a timid military salute to O'Leary and smiled at him. The man had put a hurricane lamp on a garden table. When he lit it, the sky above the clearing turned even darker. In a hearth made from large stones, he put some kindling and pieces of wood that the boy brought to him. When the fire started to take, he walked over to the cistern, took off his shirt, his trousers and his underwear. And, stark naked, he stepped over the steel edge and stood in the middle of the pool. The water came up to his waist. He placed his hands flat on the surface of the water and stared down, motionless as a statue. Suddenly his hands plunged underwater and came out holding a carp. It glimmered even in the darkness and seemed to weigh at least seven pounds.

★

He tossed it onto the grass and got out of the water. While he was getting dressed, the carp thrashed its tail against the ground and suddenly leapt as high as the cistern. When it fell back to earth, it trembled for a moment and then leapt in the air again. For several long minutes, its instinct commanded it to find water, and after one of these desperate leaps, O'Leary, sitting beside me, whispered: 'What's he waiting for? Why's he leaving it like that?'

Shivering, the man added wood to the fire. The carp twisted in the grass. The gaps between its leaps grew longer. The boy was still coming and going. He seemed to avoid looking at the cistern. Bent over the garden table, the woman was cutting tiny pieces of bread. O'Leary stood up and walked towards the cistern. When he was close to the carp, he turned towards us. Without a word, the man took a piece of firewood and threw it at O'Leary's feet. The boy and his mother looked at O'Leary as if to say: 'Don't pick it up, don't do it, it'll all be over in a few seconds.' The carp shuddered in the grass. O'Leary didn't move. The man continued staring at him. This silent combat lasted almost a minute, until I said: 'Come on, O'Leary. Come and sit down.' As he walked back towards us, the man laughingly ordered the boy to pick up the piece of wood intended to kill the carp and to throw it in the fire. When O'Leary was sitting next to me, I asked him to pass me his flask. I finished drinking and said: 'Do you want us to leave?' He heard me but didn't answer. At the foot of the cistern, the carp had stopped moving.

Now and then, the man came to stand in front of us and watched us, as if deep in thought. We stared back at him and he went away, shaking his head. Even though he had stopped feeding the fire so that nothing would remain but the embers, the flames gave more light than the hurricane lamp on the table. He said something to his wife and disappeared into the darkness. The sky was dark blue now, and the edge of the pine forest that surrounded us was black. As the crackling of the flames died down, I had the impression that unknown sounds were rising from the trees.

From where we were sitting, we could see everything that the woman was slicing on the table. In addition to the bread, there were various vegetables, onions, and aromatic herbs that we could smell from here. Only a few small blue sparks rose from the hearth now. We heard the boy speaking to the baby inside the house, constantly repeating the same phrase. The moon appeared between the tops of the trees. Coming from behind the house, the man emerged from the darkness near the cistern, crouched down next to the carp, took a knife from his pocket, and slit open its belly, provoking one final convulsion. He plunged his hand inside and threw everything that he removed into the pool. In the silence we heard the fins of the other fish beating at the surface of the water.

The man carried the carp to the garden table and began carefully stuffing it with vegetables, bread and herbs. The boy had come out of the house and watched his father's every gesture because he seemed to have a particular way of carrying them out. Sometimes he would turn to us too and his gaze would alight on O'Leary for a second before returning to his father's work. The woman started singing again inside the house and the baby sang too, in its own way. O'Leary asked: 'That's a carp, isn't it?'

'Yes.'

'So it's Jewish.'

'What?'

'If it's a carp, it must be a Jewish recipe.'

'What are you talking about?'

'I'm saying it's a Jewish recipe.'

I turned to look at him in profile.

He said: 'I swear, that's what it is. There are Jews in Lowestoft and they do it too. They come to the beach and they do almost exactly the same thing as he was doing.'

I stared at the back of the man, who was still leaning over the fish, and for an instant I thought without really thinking that the Jews must let the carp die like that too. Then I said: 'No, O'Leary, he's not a Jew.'

'That's not what I said, sir. But it's a Jewish recipe, I swear it, and I know how it's going to smell.'

'Have you eaten it before?'

'One day, the ones in Lowestoft came to see me on my dune and they brought a plate of it.'

'And?'

'I pretended to eat some and threw it all in the sea.'

'Why?'

'You'll see when you smell it.'

We looked at the table. The fish's belly was stuffed. Night had settled on everything. The orange moon shone above the pines. Moths flew around the hurricane lamp. Inside, the woman sang very softly.

The man went into the house and came back with a metal rack, which he placed on top of the stones in the hearth. He bent down to blow on the embers, and then called out. The boy, who had stayed close to the table, lifted up the fish in both hands and started walking towards his father. As he passed us, he slipped and as he tried to regain his balance he dropped the fish, which fell onto the ground with a damp flop, scattering all the ingredients that the man had patiently stuffed into its belly across the grass. The man stood up, grabbed the boy by his shirt, slapped his face and slapped it again, but it was for the carp, lying in the grass with its belly emptied, that the boy had already started sobbing. O'Leary stood up with a groan of pain and the man turned to face him, his features deformed by anger, his fist holding ever tighter to the boy's shirt, and he spoke to O'Leary in a flood of words sometimes filled with rage and sometimes with a feigned gentleness, speaking both to O'Leary and to the barrel of the rifle that O'Leary was aiming at him. Then he suddenly stopped speaking but left his hand suspended over the boy's head, and despite the shirt which was digging even more tightly into his neck, the boy was no longer sobbing but staring desperately at the rifle. O'Leary turned to me then, his eyes full of despair. His forearms were trembling and his wide-open eyes stared at me imploringly. The man started laughing and, without letting go of the boy, he raised the hand he had used to slap him a little higher and took a step towards O'Leary, who stared at me one last time with infinite sadness and the gunshot blasted the night into a thousand pieces.

I WILL REMEMBER this: the boy and his mother united for a few seconds by their silence, the mother in the doorway, dimly lit by the hurricane lamp, hand to her mouth, and the boy motionless, his face lit up by the embers, both of them silent and looking at each other, not at the man lying on his back among the vegetables, the aromatic herbs and the bread, one arm outstretched to the side, his palm turned up to the sky, almost touching the carp. The other arm, the one that the bullet hit, was trying to raise itself. The man opened his eyes and moved his lips. The echo of the gunshot, engraved in the air, seemed to come and go endlessly, like a storm circling above. O'Leary had put his rifle on the bench and was walking towards the path that ran between the pines. I picked up the rifle and caught up with him at the edge of the woods. We walked into the forest amid almost total darkness and when we came out again the stars, more numerous than above the clearing, guided us towards the road.

We each walked to one side, me by the river and O'Leary by the fields. In the darkness, the water flowed past slow and soundless towards the sea. The rifle was heavy and I ended up carrying it on my shoulder. From time to time, I would look over at O'Leary. We were separated by the width of the road. In the night he looked less stooped than in daylight. At one point I couldn't see him any more. I slowed down to wait for him, and once again we walked side by side. I kept moving the rifle from shoulder to shoulder, and I watched the dark water move away. The stars were not reflected in it but the moon was, trembling.

For more than an hour only our footsteps reverberated in the night. O'Leary's kept fading behind me and I kept stopping and waiting for him. After a while, as we were walking together, I said: 'The sea isn't far, O'Leary. Check the petrol when we get to the car and if you think we have enough left, we can try to find somewhere near the water where we can sleep. You want to try that?'

A long time after, as we were approaching the bridge and the car, I heard a word muffled by a sigh and I thought that he was murmuring an answer to himself, that he'd said yes to a question he had asked inside his head. And just as I remembered the question that I had asked him, he whispered, the words half-broken by a sob: 'Yes, sir, we can try.'